MARINADE FOR MURDER

CLAUDIA BISHOP

BERKLEY PRIME CRIME, NEW YORK

MARINADE FOR MURDER

A Berkley Prime Crime Book / published by arrangement with the author

PRINTING HISTORY
Berkley Prime Crime edition / August 2000

All rights reserved.
Copyright © 2000 by Mary Stanton.
This book may not be reproduced in whole or in part,
by mimeograph or any other means, without permission.
For information address: The Berkley Publishing Group,
a division of Penguin Putnam Inc.,
375 Hudson Street, New York, New York 10014.

The Penguin Putnam Inc. World Wide Web site address is
http://www.penguinputnam.com

ISBN: 0-425-17611-8

Berkley Prime Crime Books are published
by The Berkley Publishing Group,
a division of Penguin Putnam Inc.,
375 Hudson Street, New York, New York 10014.
The name BERKLEY PRIME CRIME and the BERKLEY PRIME CRIME
design are trademarks belonging to Penguin Putnam Inc.

PRINTED IN THE UNITED STATES OF AMERICA

10 9 8 7 6 5 4 3 2 1

For Nick

CAST OF CHARACTERS

THE INN AT HEMLOCK FALLS

Sarah "Quill" Quilliam . . . owner/manager
Meg Quilliam . . . head chef
Doreen Muxworthy-Stoker . . . head housekeeper
Dina Muir . . . receptionist
John Raintree . . . business manager
Kathleen Kiddermeister . . . head waitress
Bjarne Bjarnson . . . a sous-chef
Neil Strickland . . . producer of *Sneezer*, a guest
Mort Carmody . . . head writer for *Sneezer*, a guest
Benny Gilpin . . . staff writer for *Sneezer*, a guest
Ed Schwartz . . . staff writer for *Sneezer*, a guest
Horvath Kierkegaard . . . a Finnish financier
Everett Bland . . . attorney-at-law
Max . . . a dog

IN HEMLOCK FALLS

Marge Schmidt . . . owner of Hemlock Home Diner
Betty Hall . . . Marge's partner
Miriam Doncaster . . . town librarian
Elmer Henry . . . the mayor
Adela Henry . . . president of the Ladies' Auxiliary
Esther West . . . owner of West's Best Dress Shoppe
Howie Murchinson . . . town attorney

Myles McHale . . . sheriff
David Kiddermeister . . . a deputy sheriff
Sherri Kerri . . . owner-operator of GET
   BUFF!
Carol Ann Spinoza . . . County tax assesor
Mark Anthony Jefferson . . . vice-president,
   Hemlock Falls Savings and Loan
Andy Bishop . . . internist, Hemlock Clinic
Dookie Shuttleworth . . . pastor, Hemlock
   Falls Church of God
Freddie Bellini . . . owner of Bellini's Fine
   Funerals
Flick Peterson . . . the dog warden

IN TOMPKINS COUNTY

Bernie Bristol . . . justice of the peace
Mildred . . . a law clerk
Simon Cranshaw . . . an engineer
Captain "Dutch" Harris . . . a state trooper

PROLOGUE

"This is crap." Neil Strickland threw the videotape cassette down the length of the conference table. "Do I have to spell the situation out for you? The ratings on this show sucked last season. You had all summer to come up with a new spin. And this is it?"

The cassette spun sideways and beached on Mort Carmody's ashtray. Stubby ends of Marlboro 100s flew onto Mort's blue denim shirt and rested on the concave hollow of his stomach. He brushed the butts onto the polished hardwood floor and took a long swig from his bottle of Evian water.

At the opposite end of the conference table, Neil leaned forward and rested on his knuckles. Mort had seen meaner expressions in his lifetime; once on a burly biker in a dive bar near Laguna Beach and again on a skeletal guy just before he mugged Mort in an alley off of Sunset Boulevard. But only twice, until now. He looked nervously at Benny Gilpin. Benny was head screenwriter. He should take the heat for this shit.

Benny chuckled in an avuncular way. This was a mistake. Strickland was young. There was nothing he hated more than avuncular. Benny rubbed his eyes with a weary sophistication Neil was bound to hate even more. The producer couldn't stand attitude. Benny was full of attitude. Benny put on his sunglasses and said condescendingly, "Look, Slick."

Neil scowled. The nickname stung. He was tall, thin, elegantly dressed, eschewing Mort's own preference for California cool. Slick, Mort thought. Slicker than shit. He sighed. He could do with a drink. A stiff one. He swigged at his Evian again.

Benny plastered a "we're all in this together" look on his face and adjusted his belly over his Broad Man jeans. So he was going the reasonable route. Mort shook his head, smiling a little. The reasonable route never worked with Neil. Now, an AK-47. *That* might work with Neil.

"We got a problem here," Benny began in a friendly way.

"What's this 'we' shit, paleface?" Neil snapped. "You three over-the-hill farts have a problem. Not me. If you can't get this show in shape by week after next . . ." He drew his forefinger across his throat. "I told the network you jerks had fourteen days."

Mort looked down the table at Eddie Schwartz. Eddie's original hair color was anybody's guess. Right now it was a bottled red blond drawn back in a pony-tail, a look that worked only if you were a twenty-two-year-old hot shit, or Robert De Niro. Like the other two scriptwriters, Eddie was in his middle fifties. And their age showed, Mort thought mournfully. No matter how much time and money a guy spent on plastic surgery and laser resurfacing, it showed. Something about the eyes.

Neil, the executive producer of *The Sneezer Show!* was thirty-five but he'd already had two lifts and an eye job. Mort knew that for sure. And his *Baywatch* tan was out of a bottle. Mort was willing to bet the man's thick black hair was mainly extensions. Mort smoothed the bald spot on his own head and took another drink of Evian.

"Thing is," Benny said in an explanatory tone, "there's just too many minority groups in this country ready to complain about imagined slights. But I'm telling you, Slick, with the three of us here, you've got a good sixty years' worth of experience writing for TV right in this room. You ought to count on it. It's an asset."

Mort winced. Mentioning age was a no-no in Los Angeles. Unless you were under twenty-two.

Benny went on in a dogged, hectoring way that made the color rise to Neil's artificial hairline. "The funniest stuff comes out of making people laugh at other people. From your banana-peel skids up to Howard Stern. But you can't take that route anymore. Not with anyone who is an American." He shook his head wisely. "Too risky. 'Member the show when Sneezer dressed up like a Nazi for Halloween and had to go to the dentist? Got sued from here to East Jesus. The ADA got mad, the AJA got mad. Even the skinheads got mad." He reflected a moment. "Thing is, that was one of my best scripts. Helped a lot of kids get more comfortable at the dentist's office."

"Finns?" Neil said as if he'd found dog shit on his shoe. "So you think Finns are funny?"

"I told you," Mort said. "I told him and Eddie both. Finns aren't funny."

Strickland glanced at Mort like you'd look at snot.

"Neil, there's not enough of them to sue us!" Benny said proudly.

Neil smacked his forehead lightly. "Oh, gosh. Maybe you guys forgot." His eyes narrowed to bright blue slits and he screamed, "Who gives a shit if we get sued? Suits are good for business. Every little runny-nosed brat out there's going to watch the show if the parents are squawking about it. You should be on your knees that we get sued!" He looked over their heads and shook his head slowly. "Jesus," he said flatly. He looked at them sideways, managing to smirk with his entire body. It was the worst Bruce Willis imitation Mort had ever seen. "Now listen up," Strickland said softly, barely moving his lips. "*Sneezer*'s a kids' cartoon show. You want to turn Sneezer into a guy with a horned helmet on his head and a smart-mouthed reindeer for a sidekick, you're going to get a lot more grief than a lawsuit. You're all going to get canned. Because Finns *just aren't funny*!" He stepped away from the table and adjusted the French cuffs on his tailor-made one hundred percent pima-cotton suit. "You have two weeks to get funny. You take your fat asses and your even fatter heads on up to that retreat in—where the hell is it? Hammock Falls."

"Hemlock Falls," Mort said. He stubbed out his Marlboro. The ashtray overflowed onto his stomach again. "It's a three-star hotel in upstate New York. Hemlock Falls. Came highly recommended by the studio. Run by a pair of sisters, Meg and Sarah Quilliam. They're reopening after a bit of financial trouble, and we'll be the only guests there. We ought to get a lot of work done."

"Shut up, Mort," Neil said tiredly. "I have business in Hemlock Falls myself. And you'll get a lot of work done because I'm going to be on your sorry asses from the minute you get there."

"We'll come up with a treatment you're gonna love." Eddie Schwartz jiggled his feet up and down, up and down. He drew his wrist under his nose and sniffed. "Guaranteed, boss."

"You don't have a choice, do you?" Neil asked coldly. He opened the Brazilian mahogany door to the outside hall. "Because if you don't . . ." He drew his forefinger across his throat a second time, gave them an amiable wink, and let the door slam behind him.

"What a jerk," Benny grumbled. "That dentist show was a *damn* good way to get kids in the chair." He narrowed his watery gray eyes at Mort. "You still filling that Evian bottle with gin? Give me a hit, will ya?"

CHAPTER 1

"That cartoon's disgusting!" Doreen flung over her shoulder as she marched in the back door to Quill's office. Her gray hair frizzed behind her ears like a cockatoo's comb.

"Dor-EEN!" Dina Muir stamped in right behind the elderly housekeeper. The receptionist's pretty face was flushed. "Things are different from your day. Kids are much more sophisticated. Donald Duck just doesn't cut it anymore! They expect more . . . well, more sophistication." There was a determined set to her jaw. She looked like a cheerleader whose boyfriend had just scored for the opposing team. "I'm not trying to defend it. I'm just trying to explain it!"

Doreen made a noise like a cranky teakettle.

"Hey, guys, we're having a meeting in here." Sarah Quilliam got to her feet just in case Doreen was carrying a concealed weapon; mops and brooms were her armaments of choice. Quill didn't think the banker or the investor at her conference table would understand if the elderly housekeeper started whacking things.

Doreen ignored the four other people around the conference table and addressed Quill as if she were the only person in the room. "Baloney. I'm gonna write a letter to the network. The thing's so durn dumb it's a disgrace. What in heck did they want to go change Sneezer for? He was perfect right as he was. All dressed up in them little blue shorts and that polka-dot bow tie. He had the cutest sneeze. Why, he's practically nekkid now, except for that stupid helmet. And that accent makes him sound like some kind of a fool. Now I ast you, what kinda kids' show has a nekkid Fi—"

"It's not that bad!" Dina hissed. *"Pas devant l'étranger!"* She cast a significant glance at the only non-Hemlockian there: Horvath Kierkegaard, prospective investor in the about-to-be-purchased Inn at Hemlock Falls. And a Finn.

Quill, who had no idea what they were talking about, didn't want to know and didn't care. But the interruption had come at a good time. "We were in the middle of a discussion about food," she said.

Nobody looked at Meg, Quill's sister and the Inn's master chef. Quill ran her hands distractedly through her hair, which left it even more tangled than it had been. "Which means it might be a good time for a break." Doreen gave her a surreptitious wink. Quill made a small noise somewhere between "aha!" and "aagh." Of course Doreen had timed her irruption. The sound of the argument must have reached the rose garden, and if it had done that, then half of Hemlock Falls probably knew that Meg was on a rampage. Although Quill had to admit this rampage wasn't as fiery as it might have been, which, if she stopped to think about it, was very strange. At this point everyone in the room should have been cowering in fear. Nobody was cowering. The discussion was loud, but not nuclear.

Well, Meg was being reasonable, for her. If the current meeting went well, they would own the Inn at Hemlock Falls again, and even her volatile sister had to be happy about that.

After several nervous weeks of talks about money (not enough of it), events were falling into place. All that was left to discuss was the food.

Two of the men around her little cherry conference table got up and stretched. Mark Anthony Jefferson, vice-president of the Hemlock Falls Savings and Loan, was clearly uninterested in a discussion about cartoon characters, naked or otherwise. He walked to the small sideboard, poured himself another cup of coffee, and stood looking with a delighted smile at the plate of pastries Meg had baked that morning. The other, Horvath Kierkegaard, Finnish investor, seemed to be puzzling over whether his English was good enough to understand what he'd just heard. He stuck his hands in his pockets and rolled back on his heels.

Meg threw her pencil to the center of the cherry table and slouched into her chair, scowling ferociously. This didn't fool Quill. Meg was wearing lime-green socks. Lime green was a color Meg wore when she was in an abstracted mood. Blue socks would have been ideal for negotiations (they signaled equanimity), but Quill was just glad they weren't yellow. Yellow was the "hide under the nearest solid object" color.

"You and Doreen were watching cartoons, Dina?" John Raintree, their business manager, grinned a little and moved his long legs aside to accommodate the suddenly crowded office. It was fairly large, but Quill liked people to be comfortable. She had a long couch upholstered in red chintz scattered with pink peonies, a deceptively efficient-looking executive desk, a round conference table with six chairs, and a row of barrister-style filing cabinets, which held more art supplies than business documents.

John tipped his chair back and clasped his hands behind his head. "I thought you two were out trans-planting roses."

"We watched the cartoon before we went out to transplant roses," Dina said sulkily. "It was while we were transplanting roses that we got into the argument. Not about the cartoon, but about whether we should . . . Well, no. I'm a liar. We started arguing while we were looking for Max."

"Where *is* Max?" Quill asked, immediately dis-tracted. Her dog had a notorious tendency to get into trouble with garbage cans and chickens when he went roaming.

"Some guys in hard hats were walking around the Gorge early this morning," Doreen said briefly. "He'll come home when he's finished chasing them off. Now, look here, Quill, you gotta do something about these guys."

"What guys?" Quill asked, confused. "You mean the hard-hat guys or the duck?"

Dina said, "I'll tell them the rest of it!" She turned to Quill. "Anyhow, we were looking for Max in the Tavern Bar, because he likes to sit in there with Nate when it's hot, and Nate had the TV on, and there it was. *Sneezer*. We watched because the guys that write the show are checking in this afternoon. They sent a bunch of stuff ahead, and one of them was this demo tape." Her glance rested worriedly on Horvath the Finn for a moment. "Anyhow, I thought it might be, like, cool to, like, tell these scriptwriters we watched their show. Good guest relations, you know? But the more I thought about it, the more I realized I'd better warn you about it . . ." She trailed off and looked vaguely at the ceiling.

Horvath, who seemed to have translated Dina's ramblings satisfactorily (which was more than Quill had done), stretched to his full height of five feet two inches and said a little nervously, "Naked is not good. This Inn is for all who come, yes? Many people are not nudists in Finland."

"You don't need to worry, Horvath," Quill assured him. "*Sneezer* is a cartoon show. It's not a nudist show. We don't have nudists in Hemlock Falls."

"None?" His eyebrows rose. "No nudists at all?"

"Is this bozo the Finn?" Doreen demanded. She placed her hands on her hips. She looked like an irritated rooster. "I been on break this week. This is my first day back." Her voice dropped to a menacing warble. "I've heard a lot about you."

Quill smiled reassuringly at Mark Jefferson, who regarded Doreen in fascinated horror, then said loudly, "Doreen? Dina? I'd like you to meet Horvath Kierkegaard. As you know, he's a representative of the state government of Finland here to make an investment in a worthy American business." She frowned meaningfully and said with emphasis, "How lucky for us that he's chosen to help out the Inn."

Horvath extended his hand. Doreen sniffed disapprovingly. She owned a small percentage of their business, and had been vocal about foreigners. Dina batted her eyelashes at him, which, since she was twenty-three and extremely pretty, lightened the mood a little. Horvath beamed back at her.

In Quill's increasingly nervous opinion, Horvath's cheerfulness bordered on the neurotic. He'd been beaming when he stepped off the plane at the Syracuse airport, and he hadn't stopped beaming since. Quill's limited experience (two Finnish sous-chefs and one pastry chef) was that Finns were the Eeyores of the Scandinavian: glum, broody, and serious. They were all tall, with wintry eyes of gray or blue or pale green. A short cheerful Finn with melting brown eyes was unexpected, even disconcerting. Perhaps that's why the Finnish government had selected Horvath as chief negotiator. During the last two and a half days of negotiations Horvath had smiled a whole lot—but hadn't yet signed a thing. When Quill had told this to Doreen on the phone, Doreen had said not to trust anyone who ate herring an inch, anyways.

Quill gave herself a mental shake. She was imagining trouble. Marge Schmidt had agreed to sell the Inn back to them as long as the right kind of financing was in place. Marge had been delighted to hear about the Finns. They had a ton of money. She was so optimistic, she'd even let Meg and Quill move in early and start taking guests on a limited basis. But like all human beings with a lot of money, the Finns—or rather Horvath—seemed reluctant to give it up. That was all that was behind Horvath's skittishness about signing the agreement. Quill crossed her fingers behind her back. She hoped that was all.

"Quill? *Quill!*" Meg yelled.

Quill jerked her attention to the present.

Meg cleared her throat crossly. She tapped her forefinger on the stack of preliminary notes for her menus. "Let's get on with it. I've got to get to the kitchen for lunch."

Doreen shot Meg a beady glance under her gray eyebrows, then asked casually. "How's it goin' in here, anyways?"

"Just fine," Quill said firmly.

"We bought the Inn back yet?"

"We're getting there," Quill said. "How're you two doing in the rose garden? You probably want to get back out there and finish before it gets too hot. Don't you? I think Mr. Kierkegaard would like to see it."

Doreen set her jaw. "Got all the rosebushes back where they oughta be. What we really come in for is to ast you about them naked gnomes."

"What naked gnomes?" Quill demanded.

"You don't know about the nekkid gnomes?" Doreen asked innocently. "You all want nekkid gnomes in the rose garden, that's fine by me."

"It's a naiad!" Dina said. "That's another thing, Doreen. You don't know a gnome from a naiad. Quill told me to order naiads and naiads don't come with ANY CLOTHES!"

"Nekkid gnomes is okay by me. But if Hagar here don't want naked gnomes, and he owns, say, mor'n half of the Inn, then we gotta take them gnomes out. Because if he owns fifty-one percent, he'd be the boss. Wouldn't he?"

Quill looked at Meg, who rolled her eyes. So that's what the invasion was about. Doreen couldn't stand not knowing what was happening.

"We did *not*," Meg said tightly, "give away a majority share. We are not about to give away a majority share."

"Then you're okay, Hagar," Doreen said.

Horvath grinned at Doreen. "Horvath," he said. "My name is not Hagar, which is the name of a cartoon character extremely offensive to my fellow countrymen. My name is Horvath. And I am so glad you wish to know my opinion on the gnomes. I say . . . whatever you like is fine by me! Because, if we can settle this very small problem with the food—we have a deal!" He grasped Quill's hands in both his own and shook them vigorously. He embraced John in a bear hug. He started toward Meg, saw the glint in her eye, and backed off. "So! Perhaps we should take a short rest while Miss Meg thinks of menus. I should like very much to see these . . ." He waved his hands with a charmingly "see how my English fails me" air.

"Naiads," Dina muttered.

"Nekkid gnomes," Doreen said flatly.

"Why don't you both take Mr. Kierkegaard into the

rose garden for a walk," Quill said. "We'll join you in a moment, Horvath. And then we have a delightful lunch for you. Meg's prepared one of her best summertime meals."

"C'mon, you." Doreen opened the outside door then stood there, arms folded belligerently over her bosom. She was wearing a battered Buffalo Bills hat and a rather shapeless print dress; somehow, she invested these homely items with a guerrillalike air. Meekly, Horvath and Dina followed her into the garden.

Nobody said anything for a moment. Then Dina stuck her head back in the door and whispered, *"Quill!"*

"Not now, Dina."

"But, Quill!"

"Later, okay? Maybe after lunch. Go bat your eyes at Horvath. He likes it." Reluctantly, Dina disappeared, and Quill turned to the others. "Horvath's being a basic peach about the cash. But we've got to settle the menu issue before he gets back."

Meg began to hum under her breath. It was "Dead Skunk in the Middle of the Road." Not a good sign.

Meg was almost a head shorter than Quill. Her dark hair was cropped at the neck. In summertime, her skin turned an olive gold (Quill herself freckled in the sun) which made her gray eyes stand out. She took a deep breath and said in a deceptively calm way, "No way is some bozo banker from Helsinki going to tell me what to cook."

"Stop," Quill said. "He can *hear* you." Not to mention, she added to herself, the implied insult to their very own banker, who was biting appreciatively into

Meg's brioche not three feet away. "The rose garden's only twenty feet from here."

"I hope he *does* hear me!" Meg jumped to her feet. Her chair fell over with a crash. "I hope the son of a—"

"Meg!"

"Pizza! Burgers! Fries! In a gourmet kitchen? I don't care *who's* cooking for you. Me or Anatole Supinsky or any other chef worth a bucket of warm spit." She leaned across the table and continued with remarkable calm. "I have three words to say about junk food. For. Get. It. And that's final!"

She smiled angelically and banged out of the office through the inner door.

"It could have been worse," John said. He brought his chair to all four legs and rubbed his forehead. Quill wondered how exhausted he was. He'd been writing and rewriting the deal language in his office over his rooms in the converted carriage house. John's coppery skin—a relic of his Onondaga heritage—didn't change much no matter how he felt.

"You mean she's not really mad?" Mark Anthony said. "What's she like when she's mad?"

"She hasn't thrown anything," Quill said a little defensively.

Mark frowned. He buttoned the last button on the vest of his very elegant three-piece suit. "Quill, she may have to compromise on the food issue."

"She won't," Quill said. "But I can't believe Horvath's serious, Mark. The Inn at Hemlock Falls is famous for Meg's food. It's part of the value of the purchase price."

Mark Anthony shook his head. He'd let his hair

grow into an Afro, and the retro look definitely suited him. His smooth dark face was sympathetic. "I know, Quill. I've never in my life seen anyone as hooked on junk food as Mr. Kierkegaard. Corn dogs, McDonald's hamburgers, Taco Bell. The guy's arteries are going to explode before he signs if he keeps it up. On the other hand, I don't need to remind you that he's our chief and only investor. If the guy wants some input into the menus, he should have it."

"Not possible," Quill said. "Meg's one of the greatest chefs in the east, Mark. She's an artist. She's committed to great food. It's in her soul." Her voice rose. She waved her hands in the air. "You can't ask her to serve pizza and corn dogs. *Any*body can serve pizza and corn dogs. There's no challenge in piz—"

"Quill." John let his hand rest briefly on hers. "Mark's got a point. The Finns are ready to put half a million dollars into the Inn. They aren't even asking for a majority interest. It's reasonable for them to expect to have a little influence."

"I thought that the motivation was to establish an American base for other business," Quill said. "Half a million dollars is peanuts to these guys. Why, I read somewhere just a few days ago that foreign investors like the Finns have billions to put into American business. They're going to use the Inn's corporate status to diversify into areas where there's real profit, like farming and grapeseed oil and goodness knows what."

"Perfectly true, perfectly legitimate, and very good business," Mark said. "I've got an idea. What if we set up a separate kitchen? Turn the Tavern Lounge into a snack bar."

"Mark! This is a five-star hotel with a three-star chef!" Quill walked up and down in her agitation. "Well, it *was,* before we sold it to Marge Schmidt and she turned the rose garden into a cow corral. But the rose garden's back to being a rose garden and the Inn's going to get its gourmet rating back."

"I'd love a three-star hamburger myself," Mark said innocently. "I know, I know. The food snobs would have a fit. You'd never get your stars back."

"Exactly." Quill smiled at him. If the banker got it, Horvath *had* to get it. It was all a matter of time and diplomacy.

Mark put the general ledger and the balance sheet into his briefcase. "Look. You go talk to Meg. I'll go schmooze with Horvath. Besides, I want to see those naiads. We'll meet for lunch in half an hour, you said?"

"I did *not* tell Dina to order naiads," Quill muttered indignantly. "One naiad, I told her. To replace the one in the fountain Marge took out. And yes, we'll meet at lunch. We'd better make it an hour, Mark. Can you keep Horvath busy until then?"

"Sure."

"Well"—she got up with a sigh—"I'll go talk to Meg now." She looked at John in appeal. "I don't suppose you'd come with me?"

John shook his head. "You two need to talk. It's a couple of weeks past due. Take your time. I'm going to change clothes and take a run. And Horvath's perfectly fine on his own."

Quill made her way out of her office, across the foyer, and into the dining room. The fine old building was looking a little sparse. The pair of antique Oriental vases that used to flank the mahogany reception desk had been sold when Quill and Meg bought the Palate Restaurant. The gumwood desk looked lonely without them.

Marge—with an eye to the practical—had replaced the Axminster rug at the front door with a strip of indoor-outdoor carpeting. The Axminster was still in storage. And the leather couch in front of the cobblestone fireplace had suffered mightily from the two-day visit of a Cub Scout troop. Quill poked tentatively at a long scar in the leather.

She went through the archway into the dining room, then stood at the floor-to-ceiling windows facing Hemlock Gorge. At least the view was immune to changing owners and managers with wildly different decorating tastes.

It had been an unusually wet summer; although it was August, the waterfall was in full spate. The Hemlock River rushed over the lip of the Gorge. The sun made diamonds of the water drops, and a pale rainbow glimmered through the spray. Poplar, maples, and locust trees in full leaf spilled down the rocky slopes. In a few weeks this almost tropical richness would edge into autumn's melancholy sweetness.

Quill's fingers contracted slightly, as if she were already holding a paintbrush. She'd never tackled a landscape before. Her art had always focused on the depths of things: the irony of roses; the humid/icy heart of iris; an occasional foray into portraiture, if there was enough dissonance in the subject. Perhaps she could try to paint the Gorge in early autumn, a looking-forward-backward kind of thing.

She spread her hands and looked at them. Her fingers were long and capable. In fact, she was feeling capable all over. The Inn was theirs again. They were back where they belonged, she and Meg.

She'd walk right into their kitchen. Meg would be happily banging around her familiar pots and pans. She'd consider the addition of a snack bar without throwing too much food or denting more than one or two of the new copper pans they'd purchased

Quill felt *right* about the world. Even the suspiciously cheerful Horvath Kierkegaard would recognize her competency and sign on the dotted line, seeing the wisdom of sticking to the Inn's *haute cuisine* in the main kitchen.

The rose garden spread before her, spilling down the lawn to the lip of the Gorge. Quill eyed the rosebushes, which were still a bit shell-shocked from Dina and Doreen's transplanting. She glanced at the stone pond (still minus the naiad). Mark Jefferson was nowhere in sight. Dina and Doreen flanked Horvath Kierkegaard. Doreen loomed over him, jaw outthrust. Horvath spread his arms wide with a self-deprecating shrug, then patted Dina's posterior with a maddeningly condescending air. Quill winced. Dina's cheerleader good looks were deceptive. She was a Ph.D. candidate in freshwater pond ecology, and earned her pocket money as the Inn's receptionist. She didn't like getting groped.

Dina rolled up her sleeves. She swung. She connected. Horvath toppled into the pond. His little feet kicked feebly in the sunshine.

Quill tugged thoughtfully at her hair. She should probably go out there and explain to Dina that Europeans were woefully undereducated about certain forms of civility. She should tell Horvath that access to such American treats as corn dogs, cotton candy, and caramel popcorn required a certain amount of *politesse* not generally understood on the other side of the pond.

On the other hand, Meg probably had finished making the cold cantaloupe soup and would want an opinion on the quality of the sherry that she used.

Quill entered the kitchen in a thoughtful frame of mind. Meg flourished a wooden spoon at her. "Did you knock some sense into Horvath the Horrible?"

"Dina seems to have. He patted her posterior in a highly familiar way."

Meg smiled for the first time in a week. "What'd she do?"

"Socked him in the jaw. He fell into the pond. I came in to tell you lunch will probably be delayed."

Meg's smile broadened, which nettled Quill for reasons she couldn't quite explain. "It's not funny if it wrecks the deal."

"It won't wreck the deal. The guy's committed."

This was patently untrue. Quill's irritation with her sister surfaced. In the past week Meg hadn't mentioned once how hard Quill was working to accomplish the buyout, and she was beginning to resent it. "How do you know *that,* Karnak?"

"He bought an RV from Peterson's. On time payments."

"He did? Well, you're right. Silly me. The purchase of an RV is highly significant. Of course he's hooked." Quill sat at the worktable, immediately sorry for her bad temper. She rubbed at a spot on the stainless steel. The birch table they'd used for years had been destroyed in a terrible accident just before Marge had taken over the Inn. Its replacement was aggressively utilitarian. "Maybe we should look for a nice butcher-block counter."

"Pretty expensive," Meg commented.

"If the deal goes through, we can afford it. And I wouldn't be at all sure that this deal is solid, Meg. This guy could walk out anytime if he gets annoyed. So let's talk quietly about his lust for hamburgers."

"No." Meg picked up a whisk and began to whip an orange-colored mixture into froth. "No, I am not putting pizza and tacos on the menu."

"What about the swimming pool?"

Meg stuck out her lower lip. "I *hate* it when you do that. Okay. What does a swimming pool, which we *don't have,* have to do with hot dogs and bottled chili sauce?"

"We *can* have a swimming pool. A nice big one, just off the terrace. And if we have a swimming pool, we need a snack bar."

"Snack bar." Meg whacked the whisk against the copper bowl. Cantaloupe soup sprayed in the air. It didn't have half the attraction of the jewellike spray of the waterfall. Quill grabbed a terrycloth towel and dabbed at the spots of pale orange on her shirt. "Okay, Meg. Not a snack bar. A pool bar. Does that sound better? Even the Breakers has a pool bar. And they serve hot dogs and hamburgers and gourmet *pizza*! And it's almost the best hotel in the world!"

Meg jumped a little. She poured the soup into a glass

bowl nestled in ice, then sorted through a pile of mint leaves and selected a few sprigs. "A pool, huh?"

Horvath hadn't said a word about a swimming pool. And he wasn't going to be in a frame of mind to talk about swimming now. But the right time would show up—probably just after he'd taken his brand-new RV for a drive in the wine country surrounding the village; Hemlock Falls was hard to resist in summer.

Quill's confidence rose. Her annoyance with Meg diminished. "You know, Meggie, as long as we stick together, we can get *anything* done here. A pool would be perfect. How many times have guests asked about a pool? Ten? Twenty? Hundreds? Those TV cartoonists who're checking in this afternoon? First thing they asked about was a pool."

"They're from L.A. People from L.A. exercise all the time, when they aren't getting face-lifts. Normal people don't necessarily need a pool." Meg opened the door to the huge Sub-Zero and pulled out a bowl of fresh strawberries. They'd come from the Inn's own beds out back. She picked over the fruit with a frown, shrugged, then moved to the sink and rinsed them under the tap. She selected about a dozen of the fruits and placed them in the colander, ready to use.

Quill felt the first stirrings of genuine alarm. Doreen had picked the strawberries, a late-blooming variety that they'd experimented with a few years before. Meg flatly refused to use them for anything but jelly. "Meg?"

"What?"

"How are you using the strawberries?"

"Whipped cream. Cointreau. The usual variation on a Romanoff."

"You don't do Romanoff in August. You only do Romanoff in June for a week or two, when the berries are perfect."

"It's no big deal."

Quill could practically hear the sirens go off. "So," she said casually, "what's really up?"

Meg gave her a sidelong glance. She closed the door to the Sub-Zero, then drew a stool to the opposite side of the workbench and sat down facing Quill.

"I've set a date with Andrew. We're getting married next week."

CHAPTER 2

Quill blinked at her. "And you didn't tell me?"

Meg shook her head. She bit her lower lip, hard.

The Sub-Zero hummed. The clock on the wall over the sink clicked rhythmically. The back door slammed. The lunchtime kitchen help was here. Quill put her hand on Meg's arm. "Let's go outside for a bit."

When they'd bought the Inn the first time around—almost nine years ago now—Meg had demanded a garden. It was out back, a half acre, with raised beds and gravel paths. The strawberry beds surrounded the vegetables and herbs. The tomatoes were ripe and the eggplant bloomed purple. The air was a marinade of scents. Quill stopped at the small plot of nasturtiums and automatically bent down to pull up the latest crop of weeds.

Meg shifted from one foot to the other. She was

wearing khaki shorts and a T-shirt with a picture of a duckling on it. The duckling had a delighted smile plastered over its face and a bubble over its head that read: I'M BAD!

She said, sulkily, "I didn't talk about the wedding too much because you were so busy with the deal."

"Too much?" Quill heard the defensiveness in her voice. She kept her own response mild. For the moment. "You haven't talked about it at *all*."

"Who had time?"

"We've always made time to talk to each other."

"Look, Quill. We sold the Inn to Marge Schmidt because of the debt. We ran the Palate Restaurant for what—three months? I started cooking in New York midweek. I've done a couple of stints on Lally Preston's TV show. I'm on my way to becoming rich and famous. Well, not rich and famous. Wealthy and notorious. Okay, maybe just better off and better known. Anyhow . . . anyhow . . ." Her voice trailed off uncertainly. Sunshine caught the diamond on her left hand. "You and I talked about what would happen when I got married, we talked about it a lot."

"When you were six years old and I was twelve!"

"Oh, be reasonable, Quill."

"You're kidding me, right?" Quill clutched her hair. "This is your wedding, Meg. Your actual 'till death do us part' wedding. And you didn't say a word to me!"

"Of course I want you to be matron of honor."

"Maid of honor," Quill corrected her. "I'm not married."

"You've been divorced."

"But I'm not married now."

"You're supposed to be a virgin to be maid of honor. I don't *think* so, Quill. Now, maybe you *didn't* sleep with Daniel when you were married to him, which wouldn't surprise me one bit, if you want the truth."

Quill straightened up indignantly. "What!"

"He was *such* a jerk." Meg waved her arms. Her face was red. There were tears in her eyes. "I told you not to marry him, but *no,* you went ahead and did it anyway. So yeah, I'd buy the maid-of-honor bit if it weren't for Myles."

The sensitive subject of Myles McHale, Hemlock Falls's sexiest (and only) sheriff, was the absolute last straw. Quill flung the handful of weeds she'd pulled at the duckling on Meg's T-shirt.

"Hey! What the heck are you two doin'!" Doreen stepped between them. She brushed the dirt off Meg's shirt and scowled heavily at Quill.

"Did you know about this wedding, Doreen?" Quill demanded.

"You finally told her, then?" Doreen nodded approvingly. " 'Bout time. If we gotta find a new chef . . ."

Quill felt precisely as if someone had hit her in the stomach. "Find a new what?"

Doreen's stern eye found Meg's. "You didn't tell her everything?"

"I was going to," Meg muttered. "But she doesn't want to hear it."

Quill fought an urge to sit down and put her head between her knees. When she spoke, her voice was unnaturally calm. "So, I want to hear it now."

"I was going to, until you started throwing dirt at

me." Meg scrubbed at her face with both hands. "Oh, Quill, I'm so sorry that this got all screwed up. You know how much I like cooking at La Strazza."

"You can still cook at La Strazza during the week," Quill said steadily. "We have that all planned out. Bjarne's going to take over the kitchen here Monday through Thursday so you can train it to New York and keep the job, just as you did at the Palate."

"It's like this," Meg said. She didn't seem to notice that tears were running down her face. "Andy got an offer from the teaching hospital at Columbia to run a new pediatrics surgery. And La Strazza offered me two hundred thousand a year to take over the kitchen." She smiled through the tears. "The *Times* just hammered Anatole Supinsky for his pastries, and the management at the restaurant is petrified of the consequences. I mean, Anatole stormed out, after the review, but of course he stormed back, because what kind of chef turns his toque on two hundred thousand a year?"

"And I suppose you're going to take this full-time job?"

"Turn my back on two hundred K? To cook hamburgers? And work with *you*? This is, like, a no-brainer!"

"Were you going to leave a note?" Quill asked distantly. "Or was I just going to figure this out on my own."

"Quill!" Meg bit her lip, muttered, "I'm sorry, I didn't mean it," and started forward, arms outstretched. Quill put her hand up, warning her off. "Oh, Quillie! I can't believe this is such a mess! But there have been all these stupid plans about buying the Inn back, and

all these incredibly boring meetings. Plus, you and Myles are in the middle of breaking up, and I didn't want
to bother you with this while you were dealing with
that."

"Lay off my love life," Quill said tightly.

Meg stamped her feet and shrieked, "See? See! And
you wonder why I haven't talked to you? I *can't* talk
to you! I never *could* talk to you."

"We talk all the time!" Quill yelled.

"We squabble affectionately," Meg said, with a curious sort of dignity. "That's different. There's no content to it." She pulled up the tail of her T-shirt and
cleaned her face with it.

"That's enough," Doreen said firmly. "That there
Horvath's dried off and ready for lunch. You come in
and be nice."

"Nice," Quill muttered, *"Nice!"* She felt half a bubble off, like a level searching for a nonexistent plumb
line.

"You change your clothes for lunch, Meg," Doreen
directed. "And you, Quill, go brush your hair. It's
stickin' out all over in this heat. And I don't want to
hear a word about weddings, or accepting Anatole Supinksy's job, or movin' down east at the table."

Quill slammed into the Inn and went upstairs to
change. Fifteen minutes later, after a cold shower and
a change into clean clothes, she came back downstairs
to check the dining room before the guests arrived.

Horvath had come to Hemlock Falls Monday of that
week. Quill had scheduled one day for him to recover
from jet lag and to experience Hemlock Falls's consid-

erable charm, and one and a half days of business meetings. Which left Thursday afternoon for a celebratory lunch with Horvath and a few judiciously chosen guests. Since nothing had been signed, it'd have to be a "welcome to Hemlock Falls" lunch.

Quill had asked Mayor Henry and Marge Schmidt to join them. The mayor, because it was time for Horvath to start friendly relations with the village, and Marge because the Finns' half a million dollars was going to go straight into her pocket when the transfer of ownership was complete. Counting Meg, Quill herself, John Raintree, and Mark Anthony Jefferson, the table was set for seven.

Dina, who'd complained that the duties of receptionist were boring since the Inn was only accepting a limited number of guests, had asked to set the table. The cloth was primrose yellow. Deep gold roses floated in cobalt-blue bowls at each place setting. She'd used Quill's own sterling silver and her personal china, patterned in Kutani Crane. Quill loved the look of the china. But the exotic crane in the center of the plates seemed to have a malignant glitter in its eye in anticipation of this particular lunch.

Quill moved a salad fork three millimeters to the left. She'd changed into a long skirt and a teal scoopnecked body suit. She'd brushed her hair out and piled it on top of her head. A couple of tendrils fell in front of her ears, interfering with her peripheral vision. She felt as if red-gold snakes were stalking her. Well, maybe she was as monstrous as Medusa, if her own sister couldn't tell her she was getting married and moving away, and leaving Quill with total, absolute chaos on her hands.

John came into the dining room, moving with the easy athleticism of the long-distance runner. Quill greeted him with a watery smile. "Hey!"

"Hey yourself." He looked at the table. "Looks great."

"Dina's got a future as a decorator if she wants it. Or maybe we can train her to cook."

John's eyes were dark and his hair as black as a crow's wing. He was several years younger than Quill and, except for a two-year hiatus at a bank in New York City, had always been at the Inn to support her. Self-contained, quiet, he almost never revealed anything personal. He moved the fork three millimeters to the right. "You've talked to Meg."

"You knew about this wedding, too?" Quill's face grew hot. "I mean, do you have an invitation? *I* don't, you know. I don't even know where it is, or what Meg's going to wear." Her voice dropped into heavy sarcasm. "Tell me, John, is she registered somewhere? I should at least send her a vase!"

"Hey." John touched her arm gently. "Hey, hey, hey. Take a deep breath, Quill."

She did. Her temper ebbed.

John's tone was matter-of-fact. "How could I talk with you if Meg hadn't? This isn't really my business, Quill."

And of course, it wasn't. Of all the people Quill had met in her thirty-six years, John was the most rigidly ethical. Some of the time, like right now, she wanted to brain him for it. All of the time she depended on it.

"We'll manage through this, Quill. We'll take one thing at a time. Right now the mayor's at the front door."

Her smile was watery, but at least it was genuine. "Hmm. You red men have strange powers. From all that time in the forest, I expect."

"From seeing his van in the driveway a couple of seconds ago. And Adela's with him."

"Oh, *nuts*! Adela didn't get an invitation. I purposely didn't give Adela an invitation. What do you want to bet she asks Horvath if he eats a lot of herring?"

"I never bet on sure things," John said.

Quill laughed. "One of the things I love about you, John. You always make me—" She met his eyes and stopped in mid-sentence. He knew about her last conversation with Myles. He just didn't know what she was going to do about it. Since Quill herself didn't know what she was going to do about it, she'd buried herself in the work at hand. And ignored Meg, and bewildered Myles . . . she bit her lower lip hard.

Part of the work at hand trundled through the archway into the dining room. Elmer Henry had been mayor of Hemlock Falls for almost twenty years (excepting a short hiatus when the voters of Hemlock Falls had abandoned the routine for the exotic reaches of feminism) and put Adela, his wife, in office. Both Henrys were short, and built in a way Quill (who was inclined to the tactful) called substantial and Meg (who was not) called fat.

Mark Jefferson and Horvath followed the mayor and Adela in quick succession. Meg trailed in. Like Quill, she'd changed her clothes—to a long denim dress and pink T-shirt. Her eyes were red. She avoided looking at Quill.

There was the usual controlled confusion while everyone was seated and Quill made introductions. Quill signaled Peter Hairston, the maître d', to serve the starters. Marge wasn't here yet—but Marge wasn't known as Ten-to-Twenty Schmidt for nothing. She was always ten to twenty minutes late to meetings. It was, she'd explained, a matter of principle. Power resided with the person who made other people wait.

"You eat a lot of fish in Finland," Mayor Henry declared, after exchanging "good-ta-meetchas" with Horvath. He looked at the pâté Meg had selected as a starter with a dubious eye. "You got some ketchup for this ground-up meat, Meg?"

"Elmer!" Adela shook out her napkin carefully. "You don't ask for ketchup at a restaurant where our dear Meg is chef. Perhaps some salsa, dear? The mayor likes his meat sauced." She settled into Quill's designated seat with the deliberation of a large boat docking at a small pier. Quill raised a finger at Peter. He wiggled his eyebrows at her then quickly and unobtrusively added an eighth place.

Adela looked at the new setting in majestic disapproval. "I thought it was to be just us?"

"Marge Schmidt isn't here yet," Meg said. "And Peter? Ask Bjarne to whip up some salsa."

"I *told* you the invitation was just to me, Adela," the Mayor said. "You didn't invite her here, did you, Quill?"

"Nonsense," Adela said briskly. "Quill is always glad to see us, Mayor." Adela wore a large garden hat, one of an endless array. This one was white straw, with silk wisteria vines poking over the brim. Horvath was seated at her right. He ducked sideways to avoid the brim as she turned and looked at him. "I was telling the mayor that you eat a lot of herring in Finland," Adela said. "Do you have trouble getting regular food all the way up there?"

Horvath handled this tactlessness with aplomb. "We do not have any trouble," he declared. "What we have trouble obtaining in my country is McDonald's. Hamburgers and fries. How I love them." He sighed. Although his hair was still damp from his dunking in the koi pond, his good cheer seemed undiminished.

"Dear Meg should have taken your food preferences into account," Adela said. "I myself always try to accommodate the food tastes of our guests. What *is* it we are having for lunch, dear? Something normal, I hope. Not one of those stuffed stomach things you served us on Scots Night at that dear Palate Restaurant." Her hat brim swatted John in the eye as she turned to address Meg.

Meg didn't say anything for a minute. "Turkey," she said. "Big, fat, gobbling—"

"Rock Cornish game hen, chilled and glazed," Quill interrupted smoothly. "You'll have to tell us what you think of the orange glazing, Adela. It's one of Meg's specialties. She's perfected it over the years."

"Horned in again, Adela?" boomed a familiar voice. Quill rose and greeted Marge Schmidt with relief. The richest woman in Tompkins County, Marge was short, round, and had the eyes of a tank gunner. She sat down at the lunch table and grunted in pleasure at the sight of the pâté. Although Marge's idea of dressing for dinner was to exchange her blue bowling jacket for a red one, her taste and appreciation for good food rivaled M. K. Fisher's. "Told you yesterday at the drugstore this was a business meetin', Adela. And if you let Elmer there put salsa on Meg's pâté, I'll sit on your hat. John? Good to see you again." She nodded to Quill, grinned at Meg and Mark Anthony Jefferson, and narrowed her eyes to laser points at Horvath. "So you're the Finn with the funds," she said. She reached across the table and grabbed his hand. "Marge Schmidt. Used to own this joint."

"Ah. I read your contract to sell to the Quilliams, here." Horvath rose and bowed. "A masterpiece of clarity and financial acumen. I congratulate you."

Marge grunted dismissively, but her face flushed with pleasure. "So. You all come to terms yet? Got Horvath's signature on the dotted line?"

Horvath settled himself again. He shook his napkin out and smoothed it on his lap. "We have one stumbling block only."

"Stumbling block," Marge said flatly. "We'll take it down, then. See, in my line of work, Horvath, I like to take an ax to anything that stands between half a million bucks and me. So what's the problem?"

Quill opened her mouth to say now that the chef was going to work at La`Strazza for two hundred thousand dollars a year, there wasn't any problem at all. Nope. They could have pizza for breakfast and Hungry Man frozen dinners for entrées if they wanted. John put his hand over hers and squeezed it lightly. Quill swallowed a bite of pâté and kept quiet.

"American food," Horvath said simply. "I would like very much to see American food on the menu. Pizza, for example."

"Italian," Marge said. "Yeah? What else?"

"Hamburgers."

"That's American," Marge acknowledged. "Fries, too, I expect. Now listen up, Hagar."

"Horvath," he said firmly. "Hagar is the name of a cartoon character exceptionally offensive to my countrymen."

"Whatever. I know somethin' about the way people eat. You aware of that?"

"Of course. Mr. Jefferson from the bank has told me all about it. He told me all about the real estate in your wonderful village."

Mark nodded amiably.

"Real estate?" Quill said, bewildered.

"Perhaps this is not the correct term."

"Whatever," Marge said. "So go on, Horvath."

"I know," Horvath said, "that you ran a wonderful diner. Hemlock Diner, Fine Foods and Fast."

"That's right." Marge said.

"And that it had some of the best diner food in these United States."

"You betcha." Marge's powerful jaws made short work of the mound of curled carrots underneath her pâté.

"And that you agreed to buy *back* the restaurant the Quilliam sisters bought from you when you bought the Inn so that you could run your diner again."

Quill gave Horvath an admiring smile. Who said

there was a language barrier? He'd done a fine job of negotiating the buy-sell-buy labyrinth.

"Not quite right," Marge said. "Leastwise, I'm gonna turn the Croh Bar into the diner. I'm leasin' the Palate out."

Meg frowned. "We're going to have another gourmet restaurant in Hemlock Falls?"

"Huh-un. Combination coffeehouse and gym. Gonna get the lease signed as soon as this deal here's wrapped up."

"A coffeehouse and gym?" Adela's substantial bosom rose. "Do you mean beatniks?"

"I mean a Starbucks and exercise place all rolled into one." Marge's beady little eyes rested pointedly on Adela's loaded fork. "You could use a good gym, Adela. And so could the whole Ladies' Auxiliary. I'm gonna talk to you about memberships right away. *Any*ways." She turned back to Horvath. "Yeah, I know something about customers and what people want to eat."

"Then you would agree. There should be marvelous curly fries. Chicken wings. Triple-decker hamburgers and those sour little pickles. Tacos. And ice cream. You Americans have the finest ice cream in the world. Blueberry Crunch. Berry-Berry, which is not, as I initially surmised, a sickness from Africa. And best of all, Rocky Road, with the marshmallows, almonds, and chocolate! I love these foods, which we do not have in Finland so much."

"Hmm." Marge rubbed her nose. "I get you, Horvath. Thing is, you can buy that stuff in any little one-horse town in America. Thing that makes Hemlock

Falls different is her. You Finns got any idea how famous she is?" She jerked her thumb at Meg. "She's top of the line. I know a couple people traveled all the way from Seattle to eat here in upstate New York on account of Meg. There's more. You know how famous she is?" The thumb rotated in Quill's direction. "You take a look at those paintings in the Tavern Lounge. This is Quilliam, the artist. Know a couple of people traveled all the way from Syracuse to see her work." She laughed.

Horvath, beaming, nodded comprehension that this was a little joke. Marge continued with a confidential air. "You go to any big museum, you find a Quilliam in the corner somewhere. You don't find that in any old American town, either."

Peter removed the starter plates and placed the chilled cantaloupe soup. Quill took a large spoonful, cheered by Marge's partisanship. Of course, Marge was looking forward to a very large check for the Inn, so perhaps her enthusiasm was understandable.

"So get this, Horvath. You change the way Meg cooks you got people stayin' home in Frisco. You want burgers and fries, get yourself a swimmin' pool out back, put in a snack bar, and Bob's your uncle."

"You'll be successful," Mark interpreted. "I believe Ms. Schmidt has a point, Mr. Kierkegaard. This cantaloupe soup is wonderful, Meg."

"What kind of sherry you using these days?" Marge took a spoonful and rolled the soup on her tongue. Her eyebrows rose. "Cooking sherry? You?"

"I was in a hurry." Meg's cheeks were pink. She

rested a thoughtful gaze on Horvath. "And I didn't think it mattered all that much."

"I see it does," Horvath said anxiously. "There must be no change in the quality of the food, Meg. None. None. None. My government would be very unhappy. This would change the deal. I understand completely. The success of the Inn depends upon the chef. Mrs. Schmidt?" He raised his glass of Montrachat.

"Miss," Marge said truculently.

"I salute you." He turned to John. "Mr. Raintree, I did not realize before how much this depended on Meg. Meg? I apologize to you. I will send you two dozen roses, more beautiful than even these." His stubby fingers touched the petals of the roses in the blue bowl. "And you, Miss Meg, will learn to make gourmet hamburgers! Delicately seasoned french fries! Corn dogs that have no peer! And we will all be happy!"

Adela burst into enthusiastic applause.

CHAPTER 3

"Didja hear me, Quill?" Marge whapped her water glass with her spoon.

Quill jumped. She'd been chopping the second-best strawberries in her dessert bowl into little pieces.

"Didn't think so," Marge said. "I was sayin' as how it'd be nice if you and Meg dropped down to the new gym for a cup of coffee."

"The new gym," Quill repeated alertly. "Of course." She tugged at a stray piece of hair. "Which gym? Who owns the gym?"

"Her name's Sherri Kerri," Meg said. "She's opened up a coffeehouse with a gym in it at our old restaurant. Health food, carrot juice, that kind of thing. Marge mentioned it during the pâté."

"She's set up already?" Quill said.

"Gave her the same deal as I gave you two," Marge

said. "Thirty-day lease till the financing comes through. She don't have much in the way of equipment yet. Gonna concentrate on aerobics for a while till the business gets rolling. She's your age Meg, maybe a year or two older."

"Sherri Kerri," Quill mused. "Sure, be glad to. As soon as I get time."

"Make time," Marge said. "Soon as she gets enough women together for exercise class, I can boost the rent a little. Carol Ann Spinoza's already signed up, but she don't have to pay."

A brief silence reigned. The Hemlockians at the table knew perfectly well why Carol Ann Spinoza didn't have to pay for her exercise classes. She was the village tax assessor. She was also the nastiest human being in Tompkins County, and that included Pig Joe the hog farmer. No one said anything about Carol Ann because of Horvath, who would run into her soon enough.

"Carol Ann's taking an exercise class?" Meg asked cautiously.

"Yeah, but it's at seven in the morning," Marge said. "I figure you two can take the one at eight . . ." She blushed a little. "I'm takin' that one. And you need it, too, Adela. You get much fatter and none of them fancy hats you wear are gonna fit."

"Adela never gains weight in her head," Elmer said loyally. He folded his napkin and pushed back his chair. "C'mon, wife. We've gotta get going. Great lunch, Meg. And Hagar . . .

My name is Horvath," Horvath said. "Hagar is the name of a cartoon char—"

Elmer rolled blithely on. "I wanna see *you* at the next Chamber of Commerce meeting. Saturday morning. Ten o'clock." He cocked his forefinger in imitation of a long-defunct TV-series character. "Be there, or I should say, be here. We're holding the meetings at the Inn again, you know. So you'll be sure of Meg's good food. Aloha."

Horvath nodded and beamed. Quill was beginning to recognize the beam as camouflage. It gave the man time to negotiate the bewildering linguistic maze of colloquial English.

"You got anything on, Quill?" Marge asked abruptly. "Want to show you something about the gym right now."

"I'm not really too busy until later this afternoon," Quill said. "We've got some guests checking in around four o'clock." Too late. She stopped herself and went into reverse. "That is, John and I have a meeting . . . don't we, John?" She faltered and said in a feeble way, "You don't want to show me the gym *now,* do you?"

"No time like the present." Marge heaved herself to her feet. "Meet you in fifteen minutes at the gym. Bring your workout stuff."

"I don't have any workout stuff," Quill said.

"Then buy some. Horvath here's gonna give you enough money to buy a whole closetful of sweatpants. Esther's stocking a whole new line in her dress shop. Sherri's got a few things for sale right now, anyway. Meg? What about you?"

"Um, Andy and I are due in Syracuse, Marge." She shook her head. "Sorry, if we didn't have this meeting

already set up, I'd love to go. Nothing like a good
workout on a hot August afternoon."

"It's air-conditioned, isn't it?" Quill said.

"Sweat's good for ya," Marge said briefly. "See you
there, Quill."

"Marge, really, I don't think . . ."

Marge gave her the Look. The Look had quelled
uppity dairy farmers, recalcitrant bankers, and aggressive insurance brokers. Quill didn't have a chance.

John shook his head, smiling. "Get some sneakers,
Quill, and an old T-shirt and some shorts. I'll go with
you."

Quill sighed and muttered.

"What was that?" Marge demanded. Her head swiveled on her neck like a gun turret on a tank.

"I said, 'Fine!' " Quill shoved back her chair and
stood up. "Horvath, if you would care to come with
me, you'd be welcome."

"I am still a little jet-lagged," he said. "Perhaps tomorrow. The workout is very good for you."

"Okay," Quill said with relatively good grace, "I
give up. I'll be there. You, too, John. No backing out."

"I'm driving down." John stood up. "I want to drop
by Howie Murchison's office with the new draft of the
agreement afterward. Do you want to ride with me?"

Quill shook her head. Meg's crack to the contrary,
it was a beautiful day outside. "I'll walk. I feel as if I
haven't been outdoors for a week."

A few minutes later, walking down the drive to Main
Street, a MOMA tote bag with gym clothes in hand,
Quill realized she really hadn't been outdoors for a
week. Late-summer flowers were in full display. The

Oriental lilies near the privet hedge lining the drive had bloomed; their heady fragrance drifted in the air like petals on water. Purple chrysanthemum stood stiffly around the base of the mountain ash. Quill paused for a moment. Meg thought chrysanthemums were the most boring flowers in the world. Meg was right. She—Quill—should get Mike the groundskeeper to pull those out and plant hydrangea. Perennials were the thing; plant them once, and enjoy the flowers year after year. As long as you took care of them, perennials rarely let you down.

If she'd taken better care of Meg . . . Quill swung the tote bag against her leg. She was angry and sad at the same time. And she couldn't decide at whom she was angrier, herself or Meg. And she wouldn't look for a new chef just yet.

She turned onto Main Street. It looked the same as it always did in late summer—mellow, quiet, and lovely. Most of the buildings in Hemlock Falls were cobblestone, and English ivy grew thickly up the sides of Esther West's dress shop, the insurance office, and Nickerson's Hardware. Flower boxes of scarlet geraniums and potentilla stood against the base of black iron streetlights. Quill had never been able to paint a village scene. There wasn't enough tension in the view before her. Some of the buildings here had endured for almost two hundred years, immune to both forward and "backward" progress and the vagaries of the human beings who passed the buildings on from generation to generation.

She stopped in front of the gym. The stone building here was a good example of the village's indifference to human affairs. In the past ten years the little structure had held a Laundromat, Marge and Betty Hall's diner, Quill and Meg's own Palate Restaurant, and now a discreet silver-and-gray sign announced:

GET BUFF! SHERRI KERRI, MANAGER/TRAINER.

But the slate roof was still covered with moss, and the cobblestones made their familiar river pattern on the outside walls, as they had for the past one hundred and fifty years.

Marge opened the wooden door and poked her head out. "You made it. John's already been and gone. Signed up for a full membership. You should, too." She backed away as Quill stepped inside. The smell was unfamiliar: indoor-outdoor carpet; fresh paint; and something gym-like. Soap? Disinfectant? The mellow wood floors had been covered with a workmanlike brown carpet. Thick mats lay over that. Track lighting illuminated every corner of the former dining room. A half- dozen or more pieces of ominously professional gym equipment lined the north wall. The south wall had a ballet bar and was entirely lined with mirrors. The west end of the gym had a waist-high leather bar. The glass shelves behind it were filled with jars, cans, and packages of health food. Quill sighed. She hated health food.

Quill looked at herself in the unforgiving glass. She dabbed futilely at her hair, which was sticking up from the heat, and pulled in her stomach.

An athletic blonde of about Quill's own age came out of the back room where Meg's kitchen had been.

She was wearing a tank top, skimpy shorts, and seriously athletic-looking tennis shoes.

Marge stuck out a thick thumb. "Sherri? This is Sarah Quilliam. Quill? Sherri Kerri. Quill's the one I told you about, Sher. She's here to sign up."

"Um," Quill said. Sherri had biceps and quads that rivaled Linda Hamilton's in *Terminator 2*. She positively vibrated with good health. Quill felt a headache coming on.

Sherri laughed. "Don't look so dismayed, Quill!" She had turquoise-blue eyes and the kind of thick, springy blonde hair that Quill associated with surfers. She also had one of those perfect caramel tans like unmarred silk. "Marge has been dragging every poor soul in the village in here. I'm sure you've just come to look around."

"Not at all," Quill murmured in a confused way.

Marge clapped a large hand on Quill's shoulder. "Give her a good workout, Sher. I gotta go. I want to talk with John about how things are going with the Finn. Sher's got changing rooms in the back, Quill. Right where the Aga used to be. There's a dandy shower, too."

Quill opened her mouth to protest. Marge flexed one meaty arm. "I already worked out this morning. Feels great. And I'll see you tomorrow morning, eight o'clock for the regular class. See ya." She banged out the door as unceremoniously as she'd come in.

"You don't have to do a thing," Sherri assured her. "And you certainly don't have to join tomorrow's eight o'clock class. As a matter of fact, I've got an appointment for an eval in about ten minutes, so you couldn't work out now even if you wanted to."

"Eval?" Quill said.

"An evaluation. I always put prospective clients through an evaluation. We don't want you taking on any more exercise than you can handle at first." Her eyes ran up and down Quill's figure in an abstracted way. "You don't need to lose a single pound, Quill. Toning's the thing for you. Here. Let me show you around and explain. You can try each piece of equipment; it's a good thing you have on a droopy skirt. And I'll give you some literature on the right kind of supplement. You look a little pasty."

Quill put her hands on her cheeks. "I do?"

"Then you can come back for a free workout, see if you like it, and we'll talk about signing up then. But only if you want to."

The machines, Quill decided, were alarming. The bicycle seat was hard and skinny, rather like sitting on a pointed rock at an interminable picnic. There was something called a Thighmaster, which looked easy when Sherri did it, but which sent muscle spasms from Quill's ankles to her lower back when she tried it. The treadmill was okay, and she actually had fun on the hydraulically run chin-up machine, which did most of the work for her until Sherri reset it at a weight more appropriate to a linebacker for the Miami Dolphins.

"It's my Gravitron," Sherri explained. "You stand on this platform and grasp the overhead bars. And the machine helps you. That's it, pull up, pull up!"

Quill found herself doing effortless chin-ups. "This is fun."

"It's even better when your own muscles can make you feel like that," Sherri said seriously. "I just love this machine. It's fabulous. You have to be a little careful with the hydraulics, though. Watch it." Quill hopped off the machine and the platform shot upward with a whoosh. "It'll knock your block off. Well? What do you think? Exercise is a great stress reliever. And from what I hear, you're going through quite a bit right now."

"Stress? Me? Where did you hear that?"

"Marge. Told me there's a bit of man trouble, too. Sorry. I've been through that myself. I'll tell you, though, you should have your sister and her new husband live here and let them commute to New York. That's what Marge thinks, and the rest of the Ladies' Auxiliary."

Quill closed her eyes to control her temper and repeated her personal mantra: It's just a small town, it's just a small town, it's just a small . . .

"You okay?" Sherri asked.

"Yes," Quill said firmly. She unclenched her fists. "That's a good idea. I was going to talk to Meg and Andy about it. She's gotten a terrific job offer, you know. In New York."

"Well, I hope she doesn't leave for good! Didn't mean to get nosy, but when Marge talked me into leasing here, she gave me the whole picture, which I appreciated. And your sister's skills as a chef are a large part of it. It's not all that easy, opening a gym in a town the size of this one. But Marge seems to think your inn will be good for short-term business, and there's a nice profit in that, if you wouldn't mind my leaving flyers at your front desk." Her eyes shifted away from Quill. "Of course, I'd be glad to let you work out here for free, if you feel there should be a quid pro quo for the flyers."

"No, no, of course not." Quill blushed. "I'll sign up for a full year, and at the regular price, of course."

"That's just great!" Sherri chattered easily about the need to start slowly. "The point," she said seriously, "is to have fun and feel good at the same time. And"— she bounced behind the food bar, took down a large jar, and shook it vigorously—"this is just the ticket for your pastiness."

"I don't . . . pasty? Me?"

"This is an echinacea-based tonic out of California. And it's fabulous. You won't believe how energetic it'll make you."

"I could use a little more energy," Quill admitted.

"Exercise and these will help!" She shook the jar again, then bounced along the shelves, pulling packets, cans, and bags off them with abandon. "Here you go! There's a very good introductory price for these. You'll clarify your blood—"

"I don't think my blood needs—"

"Of course it does! Clear up your skin, help you breathe better! That stress I was talking about?"

"Well, I—"

"Perfect for that, too. And all natural." She unloaded the armful of products onto the counter.

Quill took two steps backward. "It all seems a little undignified. And—I don't know—so back-to-naturish. We've spent several thousand years getting away from eating roots and berries, as a species. I mean . . .

ground arrowroot is progress?" She picked up a plastic
Baggie filled with powder.

"You're not gonna believe what this will do for your
sex life!"

Quill tugged at her lower lip. She wasn't too sure
she needed to do anything about her sex life.

Sherri had shiny white teeth. And she smiled a lot.
Just now she was smiling brilliantly at Quill. "You
know the guy who was just in here? John Raintree? Of
course you do, he's your business partner. Marge told
me. Anyway—that's a dishy guy. He's buff, too.
Didn't think I'd find a guy like that here in the back
of beyond. Is he single?"

"Yes. And he's one of the nicest men I've ever
known." Then, to herself, she thought Idiot! She decided she could at least change the subject. "You're
not from upstate?"

"Me? No." Sherri shook her head. "Like the song
says, 'I've been everywhere.' "

"What made you decide to move up here?"

The very blue eyes looked directly at her. "What
made *you* decide to move up here?"

"Meg and I came through here on a car trip in the
spring. It seemed like Eden after New York City."

"New York City!" Sherri's eyes glowed. "That's one
place I've never been. Well, I didn't have that sort of
epiphany. It was Marge."

"Marge Schmidt?"

"Marge was looking for tenants, and a friend of a
friend introduced us by phone. Marge is pretty high on
Hemlock Falls, and she said that your inn attracted
people from all over the world because the food's so

good and you're such a famous artist . . ."

"Marge said all this?"

"Marge," Sherri said, a little impatiently. "She really likes you two. And she thinks this village is heaven on earth."

"Marge Schmidt?" Quill pinched her lower lip harder than she had before. She was beginning to sound like a parrot. She thought of all the things Marge was: bellicose, tough, "one helluva businesswoman," according to village lore. But she'd never suspected Marge of sentimentality. "So you came, you saw, you leased."

"Something like that. Beats teaching twelfth-grade English."

"Oh. You were an English teacher?"

"Yep-per as we say in the valley. I saw you blink when I used the term 'quid pro quo,' " she explained kindly. "I thought you should know that I don't spend all my time getting fit. I read, go to plays, love good movies. I even know who you really are. Quilliam, the famous painter."

Quill didn't know how to respond to this, so she didn't.

Sherri shook her head. "Even in these enlightened times, it's hard for people to say jock and literate in the same breath. Your average Joe thinks deltoids are peppermints." She glanced at her watch. Quill, who had never met anyone so self-possessed before, felt as if she'd survived a tornado. "My appointment's due right now. Do you want to set a date to come back? Tomorrow morning? The eight o'clock class? It's called Get With It and you'll have a lot of fun. And, oh, would you like to pay for your membership and the food supplements by cash or credit card?"

"I don't think Meg would be too happy about my using food—" Quill demurred.

"Nonsense!" Sherri interrupted. "I can give you ten percent off." She whipped out a calculator, tapped rapidly into it, and named a staggering sum. Quill paled. She wrote a check. The supplements alone came to two hundred and forty-two dollars and sixty-three cents.

Sherri grinned and bagged it all up. The front door opened. "And here's your appointment card for tomorrow. You know, Quill, if you want to hang around, you can see what an eval's like. I'm sure Carol Ann won't mind."

"Carol Ann?" Quill said hollowly. She turned around. "Oh. Hello, Carol Ann."

Carol Ann Spinoza nodded brusquely. The county tax assessor was the cleanest person Quill had ever met. Meg swore that she polished the bottom of her shoes and ironed her money. Her blonde hair (natural) was drawn tightly back in a neat ponytail. She smelled like pine tar soap. She had three little kids and a nondescript husband, who were as terrified of her as the rest of Hemlock Falls. "Haven't seen you for a while, Quill? You've got your C of O?"

"My what? Oh, you mean my certificate of occupancy? For the Inn?"

"Uh-huh. You can't have anybody in there until you do." The worst of Carol Ann was not her obsession with cleanliness, or even her nasty, malicious nature. It was her icy-sweet speaking voice and all the terrible things it said. Such as, "Your assessed value is up by forty percent this year." Or, "There's a pretty large fine for that." Listening to her was exactly like hearing fingernails scraping on a blackboard.

"Yes," Quill said recklessly. "I do. I think."

"You'd better make sure you have one," Carol Ann said. "I'm dropping by the Chamber of Commerce meeting tomorrow morning. I'll check it out then. There's a nice fat fine if it isn't there. Thousand dollars. Well." She smirked ingratiatingly at Sherri Kerri. "Here I am. It's so nice of you to take time for me, Sherri." She narrowed her eyes at Quill. "Sherri got a special deal for some special folk, seeing as how she's new in town. My first year is absolutely free, isn't it, Sherri?"

Sherri's eyebrows shot up. "Who told you that? The first year's membership is thirty dollars a month, which includes full use of all the machines, an aerobics class once a week, and use of the hot tub and ladies' locker room." She turned to Quill, her eyes sparkling. "But that does remind me. I've got those flyers for you. The passes entitle you to a thirty-minute workout, use of the hot tub, et cetera, and then the next visits are twenty dollars each."

Quill, who couldn't recall having agreed to the flyers, said, "Well, thanks, but—"

"Hot tub?" Carol Ann interrupted, her voice glacial. "I don't recall a license for a hot tub."

"Um, Sherri," Quill said.

"You wouldn't recall a license for a hot tub because it's none of your business," Sherri said cheerfully. "The building inspector takes care of that stuff."

"Sher—" Quill began again.

"And," Sherri rolled on inexorably, "you're going to need the hot tub if you're going to get rid of that cellulite." She reached forward and pinched Carol Ann's upper arm between two fingers. "If you've got it here, lady, I'm petrified to look at your thighs."

"Cellulite?" Carol Ann said anxiously.

"You betcha. Just at a guess, I'd say your body fat ratio is way out of line." Sherri gave Carol Ann a familiar smack on the rear. "Get into your workout duds, pal. We'll see what you're made of."

"And that was that," Quill said to Meg and Andy a half an hour later. She set the bag of food supplements on the steel worktable with a thump. "I gave the flyers to Dina and she set them out on the reception desk. It was worth buying this stuff just to see Carol Ann get flattened."

All three of them were in the kitchen. Quill had walked back to the Inn with a light step, despite the thousand-pound bag of herbal junk food dangling from one arm. "A complete and total rout."

Meg waved her chef's knife in the air. "Hah! Carol Ann and her comeuppance! I wish I'd seen it!"

"You would have seen it if you hadn't fibbed about your trip to Syracuse," Quill said. "You could have come with me and seen it yourself."

"What's Sherri like?"

Quill thought a moment. "A steamroller." She took a deep breath. "She had an interesting perspective. You know, apparently there's been talk of you leaving Hemlock Falls, Meg. As a matter of fact, it's great that both of you are here right now, because I want to talk—"

"Oh, no!" Meg drummed her wooden spoon on the stainless-steel worktop. "No gyp club for me."

"Meg! It is not a gyp! And signing up for exercise class is not what I wanted to—"

"I'll pass. I get more than enough exercise slamming around this kitchen all day. And you've got a hope if you think I'm stuffing my insides with that herbal stuff. Besides—"

"Besides, you'll be in New York City a lot," Quill put in easily. "*I'm* going to sign up. I might even try some of this stress-reducing powder, or whatever it's called. And speaking of living in New York . . ."

"You left a check, didn't you? You've already signed up. She bullied you into it right there! Quill, you sucker! How much?"

"I don't get nearly enough exercise around here. And I'm getting sort of spongy."

"How much of a check did you leave?"

"Meg!"

"I'd just like to point out that we haven't signed with the Finn yet, and at the moment the old bank account is about zero dollars."

"Three hundred bucks. But I'm going three times a week, plus the aerobics class."

"In a pig's eye."

"I am," Quill said heatedly. "If I go three times a week plus the aerobics class, it works out to like three dollars a hour or something. A bargain," she added sententiously, "when one's health is at stake."

"And the herbal crud?"

"Not that much," Quill fibbed.

"You know very well the best thing for your body is fresh food. Not stuff that's been packaged up in some godforsaken place in the Himalayas. I'll bet the filler's yak dung."

"I'm taking the supplements back," Quill said. "So lay off."

"What a racket." Meg grinned and took off the cloth draped over the top of the bowl containing her sourdough starter. "Listen. Make sure Bjarne checks this while I'm in New York, okay? It needs a few more days, but it's iffy how long because of the heat."

Meg seemed in an approachable mood. It was the time to work this thing out. She glanced quickly at Andy Bishop. The doctor was just slightly taller than Meg, and had the lean, compact build of a professional tennis player. He was quiet, and didn't react at all to emotional Sturm and Drang. He was a great partner for Meg.

"I know Sherri offers family memberships," Quill said casually. "If you two lived here and commuted to New York, rather than the other way around, maybe we could all join." Meg frowned.

Andy shook his head, smiling. He patted his flat stomach ruefully. "I've already taken a membership in a city gym."

Meg's frown developed into a scowl. She stared defiantly at Quill.

"Well. Let's talk about that." Quill settled herself onto a handy stool and took another deep breath.

The door to the kitchen swung wide, and Dina Muir poked her head inside. "Quill?" Dina's unnaturally high-pitched voice broke Quill's train of thought.

"We've got a little problem. The guys from L.A.—"

"Guests," Quill corrected automatically. "Did you show them the flyers from Sherri's gym? It's our latest guest feature."

"Yeah, but they just got here. So, like, I really need to talk to you."

"Okay," Quill said in a bewildered way.

"Out here! In the dining room! You can see them from here!"

Meg shrugged and turned to the sink. Quill followed Dina out into the dining room. She could see the foyer through the arched entrance. There was a confusion of people.

"It's Sneezer, you know!" Dina whispered urgently, "I've been trying to tell you! They've turned him into a Finn!"

Quill rubbed her nose, sorting this out. "Sneezer's a cartoon," she said. "And the character's a Finn?"

"They changed it!"

Quill didn't ask what she meant. Quill made it a practice never to try to follow Dina's erratic thought processes. Doreen's opinion was that Dina was too smart to talk plainly, and the opinion had merit. Dina was all-but-issertation at Cornell University. She only really focused when the conversation revolved around coecephods, which it rarely did.

"They'll have to meet Horvath, then," Quill said cheerfully. "He might get a kick of it."

"Quill, just give me a second in private, okay? I mean, not only is Sneezer a Finn, but the sheriff's in the lobby."

"Myles?" Quill said, her voice going up a bit. She

patted her hair. She would *not*, she told herself firmly, check to see that she had any blusher on. She was suddenly aware of John's quiet presence at her side. "Tell him, Myles, I mean, that I'm a little too busy to see him now, and I'll give him a call later."

"He's not here to see you," Dina said.

"Hey! Dina!" A burly man in a sloppy denim shirt and wrinkled khakis signaled Dina from the archway. "Where'd you get to, kiddo? We're getting a speeding ticket even as we speak."

"This is Benny Gilpin. Benny, this is my boss, Sarah Quilliam. And my other boss, John Raintree."

"Yo," Benny said. He had a bushy gray beard and watery gray eyes. He didn't look like a person from Los Angeles at all. He looked like a farmer from Tompkins County. Quill smiled at him. He gave a dismissive snort. "Hey. I could use a hand in here." Farmers from Tompkins County were a lot more courteous. She set a smile firmly in place.

Quill, John, and Dina followed Benny into the foyer. There were too many people in it. There was a gray-faced, cadaverous man with a bald head, a cigarette hanging from his lip, and an ash-covered denim shirt. The man next to him was pudgy, with bleached-blonde hair drawn back in a ponytail and furtive little eyes. A third figure hung back by the staircase, under the stairwell.

All of them were dominated by a tall broad-shouldered figure in uniform.

"Hello, Myles."

"Quill." He nodded equably at John. His eyes were steel-colored and his hair dark, with a streak of gray through the forelock. He'd recently resumed his job as the sheriff of Tompkins County after a yearlong stint as an investigator for an internationally based security firm. Before that, he'd been a lieutenant in the NYPD. For the past six years Quill had loved him. She didn't anymore.

All of this was written in his face, and more.

Quill didn't look at him directly. She glanced at his chin, with that big, insincere smile on her face. She faced the group of incoming guests with that same smile, and wished she were in Detroit. Or Tuscaloosa for that matter. Anywhere but smack in the middle of an incipient brouhaha with a former lover as the pivot.

She swung into innkeeper mode: professional, capable, and competent. She'd had a lot of practice over the years. "Now, how can I help you all?"

A tall, slender man removed himself from the stairwell and joined the group clustered by the cobblestone fireplace. Quill cataloged the suit: olive-green Armani. The haircut: extensions, with gray dye at the temples. The sunglasses: French. The attitude: ain't I cute. His gaze slid over her. "Hey," he said, which Quill surmised was the L.A. version of "How do you do?" "I'm Neil Strickland. And you are?" His violet-blue eyes crinkled at the corners.

"Sarah Quilliam."

"Well, Sarah, it's like this." One corner of his mouth quirked upward in a smile. He put his hand on her bare arm and ducked his head so that his mouth was near her ear. "You see our Benny?" He cocked his eyebrow at the khaki-shirted guy. "We're in this rental car, and Benny's maybe going a leetle bit faster than our back-

woods boy here"—he nodded in Myles's direction—
"can tolerate. Miss Dina, there, tried her cute little best
to talk our boy out of giving us a ticket, but . . ." He
shrugged. "She thought you'd have a better shot at it."
He smiled. His teeth were capped. His eyes roved over
her again. "I believe it."

Quill's dog trotted in the open front door before
Quill could give in to the almost uncontrollable impulse to break the innkeeper's first commandment.
(Don't Belt the Guests.) There was general revulsion
at the dog's appearance. Wherever Max had been, he'd
been out rolling in it. Just what he'd been rolling in,
Quill couldn't determine; it was gluey, redolent of car-
rion, and very brown. It was all over him.

Max had gained quite a bit of weight since Quill had
rescued him from starvation earlier in the year. Dina
estimated him at close to a hundred pounds, although
even Quill couldn't get him to stand on the bathroom
scale, so no one knew for sure.

Max stopped short and surveyed the assembled party
with his head cocked to one side. He saw Myles, whom
he liked, and his tail started to wag.

Max pattered farther into the lobby. Everyone
moved back, like a herd of ducks avoiding an oil spill.
Dina started to call a futile "here, boy, here boy." Two
of the scriptwriters—the smoker and the aged adoles-
cent—made for the stairs. Benny of the khaki shirt
stood on the couch. Strickland stepped nervously behind Quill.

Max extended his forepaws, stretched, and gave
Quill an idiotic grin. Tail wagging furiously, he trotted

happily around the foyer, sniffing furiously. Dina made a dive for his collar. Max skipped aside.

Quill considered her dog for a long moment. Then she turned and whispered into Neil's ear, "That's the sheriff's dog."

"Jesus. What a piece of shit."

Quill widened her eyes. "Don't let him hear you say that! Keep your voice down! He thinks the world of that dog. A man like you should be great with dogs and kids. If you gave Dina a hand in catching him, then pet him a bit, it'd go a long way toward brightening the sheriff's mood. He's got a soft spot for anyone who likes dogs. And I'll do the rest."

Neil didn't look directly at Max. His face was twisted into the sort of expression kids had when they said, "eeeww." "Thing is," Quill confided, "the last speeder Sheriff McHale caught gave him a little grief and . . ." She shrugged.

"And what?"

"No one's seen him since." She narrowed her eyes in Myles's direction. "I've heard the sheriff is heavily into the survivalists. Happens up here, you know. There's supposed to be quite a large group of them back in the woods. No one knows for sure."

Meanwhile Dina had successfully backed Max into the umbrella stand by the front door, then tried to shoo him out without getting her hands on him. Max's tail thwacked against the pottery stand with a *thump-thump-thump*. Brown goo flew into the air with each thump. He looked very pleased with himself.

Neil took an umbrella out of the stand and gingerly poked at Max with the handle, which, although the act itself was not what Quill had anticipated, delivered impressive results. Later Quill was to reflect on two things: first, most people would have approached the dog courteously. They would have crouched down and said something along the lines of "here, doggie, good dog." Max was a genial creature. He would have assumed such pleasantries were an invitation to a doggie hug. This would have cost Quill a dry-cleaning bill, but she would have paid three times that to see the smarmy Neil Strickland in his Armani suit covered with crud. And it would have made Myles laugh.

Second, in her own defense, she had no idea that Max's mysterious past must have included an unpleasant encounter with an umbrella.

The dog went straight for Strickland's throat. It was a head-on, no-foolin' leap that knocked Strickland backward over the leather couch and into Benny. The eeriest part was the dog's silence. His jaws closed around Strickland's shirt collar with no warning growl at all.

Strickland screamed. It was a high, pure squeal of terror that made Quill's skin crawl.

Myles and John reacted simultaneously. Myles grabbed the dog's throat. John, who was quick, put both hands around Max's muzzle and held it shut. Quill found her voice and shouted, "Max! *Down!*"

Max stopped wriggling. John and Myles held him fast. Quill ran to the couch. She heard Dina dialing for an ambulance and called out, "He's fine. No blood."

"Shocky," Myles commented, and he was right. Strickland's face was pale under his bottled tan. His eyes rolled up, showing the whites. He gasped for breath. "You might give Andy Bishop a call, Dina."

"He's in the kitchen with Meg."

"Then get him, please."

Quill looked into Max's eyes. Whatever rage had possessed him was gone. "He's okay," she said.

Myles nodded to John. They released their hold on Max. He leaped away, then whined and bumped Quill's knee with his head.

"Jesus," Strickland moaned.

Max growled.

"John," Quill said. "Could you take him out? Ask Doreen if she'll bathe him."

John grabbed the dog's collar and led him out of the foyer. Quill looked guiltily at Myles. "Strickland's fine, you know. His shirt's torn. But there's not a mark on him. He doesn't need Andy."

"You might, if Strickland decides to sue."

Quill bit her lip. "You're right. Thanks. Appreciate you looking out for me."

Myles smiled a little. "Us survivalists take care of our wimmin."

"You heard me!"

"As you say, I appreciate the gesture." He glanced at the couch. Benny hauled Strickland to a sitting position and began to pat his face. "Slimy sort of fellow, Quill. But isn't there an innkeeper's rule about setting the dogs on the guests?"

"Yes," Quill said, shamefaced, "but I had no idea Max would leap on him. He's never done that before, Myles. You don't think he'll really sue us, do you?"

"Strickland?" Myles shrugged slightly. "We'll work something out. Maybe before I leave to bury the body of the unfortunate speeder I caught before him."

"Myles, you don't have to bend any principles for me." She knew this was the wrong thing to say. She'd known it before it was halfway out of her mouth. Myles's frown was immediate.

Andy came in, followed by Meg. Quill explained briefly, then left, ostensibly in search of Mort and Eddie, who had prudently disappeared the moment Strickland screamed. There wasn't anyone in the lobby she wanted to talk to. Not Myles, not Meg. Especially not the even-tempered, perfectly nice doctor who was going to marry her sister in a week.

She went out to the rose garden. The Tavern Bar would be the first destination of any scriptwriter worth his salt. But she needed time to think. So she walked restlessly around the koi pond, kicking idly at the roses.

Marge had allowed some Texas Longhorn cattle to take up residence in a makeshift corral there. She'd been practical enough to transplant the more valuable of the bushes to the south side of the herb garden out back. Some of these Doreen and Dina had already brought back. Those that had remained in place were the Princess roses and the climbers such as Blaze. Texas Longhorn cattle would eat anything, and they had thrived on the thorny branches. But the climbers were tough, and the stunted bushes would be fully recovered next spring.

Next spring. Where would she be next spring? And with whom? Would Meg and Andy visit on holidays? Would Myles turn to one of the endless parade of single women from Cornell who thought his laconic style a cover for . . .

What, exactly? A man who could look at a painting and see the allusions to earlier works in it? A man who found shades in color—not absolutes? Who had a sense of place, this place, the Inn.

Is that what she wanted in Myles? Qualities he didn't have?

Quill walked to the gazebo overlooking Hemlock Gorge and went inside. She turned the rocking chair around and faced the Inn. It was a huge, sprawling building, with a copper roof and slate terraces. There were twenty-seven rooms, two suites, and a dining room, which could handle one hundred and forty. The dark green wood shakes had to be painted, repaired, attended to, every year.

She knew she loved the old building. It cupped the ground beneath it like a comforting hand. It held her.

She'd made a mess of the finances the first time around. Mostly because she hadn't listened to John. He'd tried to warn her.

She'd almost lost it. Now she'd made a mess of her relationship with her sister. She poked her toe moodily at a clump of day lilies. She'd ignored the signs these past few weeks. To be absolutely, ruthlessly fair, Meg had made three attempts to sit down and have a serious talk. Three that Quill could recall; there had certainly been more that she'd overlooked.

And as for Myles . . . Quill's mind sheered away from Myles.

Max bounded out of the French doors leading to the

Tavern Bar. His fur was wet from a hasty but thorough scrubbing. He raced into the gazebo, ears flying. Then he skidded to a halt and shook himself hard. Quill bent out of the way of the lemon-scented spray. Waving his tail in an invitation to go for a walk, Max barked twice.

"Not today, Max. No time." She looked at her watch. "Three-o'clock, Max. I have responsibilities, you know."

His ears flattened. He looked longingly at the woods beyond the Gorge. With a heavy sigh, he picked his way to the grass and rolled vigorously. Then he curled himself into a ball and put his nose on his paws, watching her.

Quill sat down beside him and stretched her legs out in the grass. "My personal relationships are all screwed up, Max."

He sat up in alarm. Quill scratched his ears. "There's a common element to each and every one of these messes, Max. The mess with Meg, with John, with Myles. Want to know what it is?"

Max panted. His breath was awful. He'd probably eaten a bit of whatever he'd rolled in.

"Me." She bit her lower lip hard, but it didn't help. She moved into the shelter of the gazebo and curled up into the rocking chair. She cried, drying her nose on the hem of her favorite challis skirt. And then she fell asleep.

She woke when a shadow fell across her face. She blinked. John stood over her, her face blotting out the sun. Max was a heavy weight on her lap. She had that fuzzy-headed thick feeling that meant she'd been hard asleep for a long time. She sat up a little dizzily and pushed Max to the floor. She looked at her watch. "Five-thirty!"

"So this is where you got to. Are you all right?" John sat in the chair opposite her, drawing it close enough so that Max, whose chest and belly lay across her ankles, could put his head on John's feet.

"Yes. Sure. I must have fallen asleep! How's Mr. Strickland?"

"I haven't seen him for an hour or so. But he was fine. Physically, at least. He seems to have a phobia about dogs. God knows why he tried to corral Max."

Quill twiddled her thumbs.

"Myles had a talk with him. I don't know how much good it did. Pointed out that Strickland couldn't have chosen a better way to get out of a ticket."

"Maybe we should let them stay at the Inn for free."

John raised his eyebrows slightly. "I thought one of our new operating principles was that I'd handle billing decisions. And this wouldn't be a good billing decision."

"Okay. We charge them, same as everyone else."

"They're already getting a reduced rate since we're not officially open."

His shoulder was just touching hers. Quill bent down and shoved Max off her feet. When she sat back, she'd moved just enough to avoid the physical contact. "I had a fight with Meg," she said presently. "Are things in as big a mess as I think? I mean, good old Marge, with the best of intentions, went ahead and convinced Horvath that he'd be making a mistake to invest without Meg here as chef."

"We'll have to see."

"We can't sign the contract without telling Horvath she's leaving."

John made an impatient movement. "Of course not. I don't think she's actually leaving, Quill. As I understand it, she's going to live in New York during the week and commute here for the weekends."

"That's not what she said today."

"She was angry today. She'll come home, Quill."

"How long do you think it will last? She's making a home there, John. It'll be impossible not to."

"I think we should cross that bridge at the proper time. And you're avoiding the real issue, Quill."

The final phrase of his comment hung unspoken: "as usual." "So is that why I've screwed up everything? Because I keep avoiding the real issue?" Tears threatened again. Quill pinched her nose, hard.

"You haven't screwed up everything."

"Oh, no," Quill said bitterly. "My sister can't, won't, *didn't* tell me she was getting married and moving to New York. And as for Myles—" She stopped herself. John had left his job as business manager for a lot of reasons, but the most important one had been Quill herself. She wasn't about to talk about her screwed-up relationships with someone with whom she had a screwed-up relationship. "Never mind."

"What do you want, Quill?"

"What do you mean?"

"Exactly what I asked. What do *you* want? You want the Inn back? We're working that out. You want your sister's love and respect? Do you want me in your life? Or Myles? Do you want to have the time to paint? You need to work all those things out. But you can't if you don't know what you want. Quill, look at me." He put gentle hands on her shoulders. Whatever he saw in her face made him take his hands away.

"Okay," he said after a long moment.

Quill rose to her feet and brushed her skirt off. "I'm going to wash my face." Then, politely: "Are you going to be around for dinner?"

"Possibly. I came out to find Max. I need the ID number off his collar to pick up his rabies certificate from the vet. And Strickland wants a blood sample to see if Max has any kind of infectious diseases."

Max knew the word *vet*. He stood up and wandered casually to the edge of the Gorge.

Quill made a sound like "phuut!" "Max doesn't have any diseases. He's as healthy as a horse. Aren't you, Maxie?"

Max barked at the sound of his name. He was, Quill admitted, possibly the world's ugliest dog. His bath had removed the stinky goo, but nothing could improve his coat, predominantly a mixture of ocher and dull gray. He was disheveled and ungainly, with floppy ears. He almost always smelled of something awful. Quill regarded him affectionately. Theirs was one relationship she hadn't screwed up. There was nothing like the love between a woman and her dog. "Bite 'em like you sees 'em, Max," she muttered. "Yay for you."

"If you're going to encourage him, you'd better keep multiple copies of the rabies certificate handy. Strickland insisted on filing a dog-bite report. Most people would. And he's got a point, Quill. He wants to be sure the inoculation's current."

"He could take my word for it," Quill muttered.

"Don't you dare laugh. I didn't have any idea Max would go for him like that, John. Strickland was just so . . . so . . ."

"Offensive? Obnoxious? Oleaginous?"

"Orful. As in"—she tried on a Cockney accent— " 'Ain't it orful, judge?' Okay, we'll get his ID number. I'll try and hold him while you read the tag. Come here, Max." She patted her thigh.

Max grinned and danced backward.

"Uh-oh," Quill muttered. "It was the V-E-T word. That right on top of the B-A-T-H is going to make him impossible to catch."

As if on cue, Max dashed over the edge of the Gorge and was gone.

John swore. Quill groaned. She called "Max" a couple of times, then "walk?" in a sprightly way and "kibbles" before she gave in to the inevitable and plunged after John to bring the damn dog home.

It was not an afternoon for tramping through the woods. For one thing, she had her sandals on. For another, it was getting hot. They'd been lucky, this August. Late summer in upstate New York was almost always a stinker, hot and humid. But the unusual rains had kept things cool.

Until today, of course. John moved lithely ahead of her, somehow avoiding the brambles, the sticker burrs, and the roots, which reached for her big toe one too many times.

"I curse your Indian ancestors," she shouted after him. "Slow up a little, John!"

She caught a flash of his smile. She hollered "Max!"

more to relieve her annoyance than any expectation of having the dog bounce home.

Max answered with a series of sharp, excited yips. Quill grumbled to herself. She knew that bark. He'd found something wonderful to roll in again. And, dammit, that meant another bath.

She slipped down the gravelly slope to the shore of the Hemlock River. The Inn loomed above, casting a shadow on the ground. She saw her dog, dancing in excited circles at the water's edge. And John.

She knew something was very wrong by the set of John's shoulders. Even before she saw the body.

CHAPTER 4

"Max didn't roll on the corpse," Andy assured Quill.

"Do you know for certain? How stupid. Of course you do. You saw the body." Quill ran her hands through her hair. "He checked in three hours ago, Andy! How could someone have killed him in three hours! No one knew he was here!"

"We don't know that anyone did kill him, Quill."

They were standing at the river's edge, waiting for Myles and the forensic team from Syracuse. After Quill had raced back to the Inn to call the police and the ambulance, she and Meg had roped off the area around the corpse. Max, in highly vocal dismay, was locked in the garden shed. Doreen and Dina were up on the lip of the Gorge, preventing curiosity-seekers from scrambling down the slope to the scene.

They were all used to the routine after—how many

cases was it now? Seven. That was it. Seven cases of murder. And this was the eighth. Quill didn't need Andy to hedge about whether this was murder. Someone had killed Neil Strickland. Someone had laid the back of his head open with either an ax or a machete. Quill wasn't sure where the murderer had found a machete in upstate New York. Which might be a clue, if it *was* a machete and not something else with a brutally sharp edge.

"Quill?" Andy looked at her, his brow furrowed. "Are you all right? You look a little green around the gills."

"She's going to be sick," Meg said briskly. "She always looks like that just before she's going to york."

"You don't look so hot yourself," Quill retorted.

"You're shivering," Andy said.

"It's cold down here!"

"It's eighty-five in the shade," Andy said kindly. "Sit down, Quill. Put your head down."

"I know, I know." Quill sat down and put her head between her knees. She felt a little better. That was the trouble with Andy Bishop. If Meg was going to run off and marry a doctor, why couldn't it be a nice rude orthopedic surgeon or an icy pathologist? Those guys she could hate. Nobody could hate a short, compact blond internist with a specialty in pediatrics, a heck of a tennis serve, and a kindly, if distant, manner.

Meg sat down next to her and put her arm around her shoulders. "How's your stomach?"

"Okay."

"And what are you mentally rambling on about?"

"Rambling on about?"

"Yes, Quill. It's how you handle stress. You go all

vague and spend a whole lot of time thinking about irrelevancies."

Quill was too tired to squabble. And she was tired of quarreling with Meg. "I was thinking about how nice Andy is."

"Yep. He is. A genuine sweet patootie."

"Sexy, too," Quill observed.

"Hands off my man," Meg said lightly. "Oops! Here's Myles."

Myles listened quietly to both John's and Quill's account of finding the body, then sent them back up the hill to the Inn to his deputy, Davey Kiddermeister. "He's set up in the bar. Give him as complete a statement as possible," he said. "You know the drill by now." He bent over and looked into Quill's face. "Are you all right?"

"Fine."

"Get something from Andy to calm your stomach. How long has it been since you've eaten?"

"Really, Myles, I'm perfectly fine."

"I'll want to speak to you before I leave."

Quill nodded, feeling as she always did around Myles: a little helpless; hemmed in; fixed in place. "I'll wait," she said. Which was the biggest problem. She was always waiting for Myles, putting the rest of her life on hold. And there was always something else, urgent, compelling, necessary, that he'd been called away to do.

"But you don't *need* to wait!" he'd exploded, when she'd explained, weeks ago, that she couldn't spend her life on hold. "Get on with your work, Quill. Just let me be there when I can."

Quill sighed shakily, and followed John up the hill to the Inn.

The short, arduous climb was enough to clear her head. By the time she entered the Inn through the Tavern Bar, she'd shoved the shock and confusion aside. Benny, Mort, and Ed were slumped at the long mahogany sweep of the counter, in close conversation with Nate the bartender.

Davey Kiddermeister sat stiffly at one of the larger tables, his ears pink with excitement. Davey was twenty-eight. His law enforcement career was hampered by the fact that he had a smooth, cherubic face, hair so blond it was almost albino white, and a blush that deepened in direct proportion to the emotional intensity the job demanded. Davey blushed pink when he stopped speeders and crimson when he had to arrest somebody. Right now he looked like he'd spent three days in the Arizona desert without a hat.

Quill sat down at Davey's table. John stood at her back.

"Sorry, Mr. Raintree. Have to interview the eyewitnesses separately. Could you sit somewhere else?"

John went to the bar and sat down with the three scriptwriters. Judging from the ashtray in front of Mort, they'd been sitting there since they tried to check in at three o'clock.

Quill gave a succinct summary of discovering Mort's body, then added, "We weren't eyewitnesses, Davey. We just found the body. Actually, we found Max. Max was the one who found the body."

"That dog's getting pretty good at it," Davey said, referring to a case Quill and Meg had investigated several months ago. "I was just sitting here, thinking that Max would be a big plus at the sheriff's department. I could, like, take him out and he could find more of 'em for me. Save you the trouble."

"It'd work if we were in Bosnia," Quill said gravely. "But you might end up wasting a lot of time around here."

"Thing is, I like Max," Davey said simply. "And if you get Howie Murchison to represent Max, I'll bet old Howie could cut a deal. Max wouldn't have to be put down."

Quill stared at him, openmouthed. "Stop," she said. Davey stopped.

"What in the world are you talking about?"

"Well, the guys from L.A. think that Max did it. Killed Strickland, I mean. They called Flick Peterson down to the dogcatcher's offices and he came and took Max to the pound. They're going to get a court order to have Max put down, which is why," Davey concluded, with an air of long-suffering patience, "I told you that Max would be better off with me."

"David!" Quill's shout quieted the bar. She clapped her hand over her mouth and muttered, "Idiot-idiot-idiot."

"Pardon?" Davey said.

Quill took a deep breath. "Look, Deputy. A sharp-edged instrument killed Neil Strickland. An ax or a machete. There isn't a single dog bite on that body. I looked. At all of it."

"Strickland was terrified of dogs. They figure Max went for his throat when he went out for a walk and that he was so scared he fell and sliced his head on a rock."

"Strickland went for a walk?"

"After Max attacked him the first time." Davey licked his thumb and paged through his notebook. "Says right here. Statement by Benny Carmody, taken by me, David Kiddermeister, deputy, village of Hemlock Falls, Tompkins County, this date. Benny says: 'Neil was really shaken up. You could tell he had a real problem with dogs. We had a couple of pops in the bar. Didn't help Neil's jitters at all. Then he made a couple calls on his cell phone, but he just couldn't settle down to work. He went upstairs and changed into workout clothes, then he came back and said he was going out for a run. Said only thing worth seeing other than the damn redhead that ran the damn place'—that's you, Quill, sorry, but it's written right here, just like that—'was the damn waterfall. The last I saw Neil, it was about a quarter to four. He headed out the French doors to the terrace.' That's the full statement, Quill."

"Where were the others?"

"The other what? You mean Mort, Ben, and Ed?"

The Three Stooges, Quill thought, but she held her tongue.

"Drinking in the bar. Well, Mort went up to his room, but came back after about an hour. Said his stomach wasn't too good." The deputy leaned forward. "Nate says the guy put away three gin martinis in less than ten minutes. My stomach wouldn't be too good either."

Well, Deputy," Quill said icily, "I was out by the Falls in the gazebo until five-thirty, and I didn't see a thing. I would have heard a terrorized scream for sure. Not to mention the sound of a hundred-and-sixty-pound man falling down the slope to the river."

Davey paged through the notebook. He found his place and moved his lips, reading. He looked up and said, "You were asleep."

"I would have heard Max attack Strickland," Quill said with asperity.

"According to the eyewitnesses of the first attack . . ." Davey started to flip through his book.

Quill grabbed his hand. "Just *tell* me," she said tightly.

"Max just jumped the guy. Didn't bark or growl or nothing. Mort said the dog actually went after him in the foyer."

"Are you sure that Mort can tell the difference between a dog and a pink elephant? I was there in the foyer, David. Max didn't go near Mort. As a matter of fact, Mort and his pal Ed beat feet the minute their boss started screaming."

"Nate did say the two of them came into the bar first about twenty after," Davey admitted. "But that was two hours before Strickland bought it. Doc Bishop says Strickland wasn't more than half an hour dead when you found him. And Doreen said Max finished his bath around five. Which would have given him plenty of time to run out and kill—hey!"

Quill shoved her chair back. She was so mad, the room was beginning to sway before her eyes.

"Where're you going?" Davey said anxiously. "Quill!"

Several more deep breaths didn't do a thing to quell

her tearing rage. She marched over to the bar and
grabbed the nearest figure. There was a shout of protest. The red mist in her brain cleared; she had Ed
Schwartz by the ponytail. She shook him so hard, his
head rolled. "I want my dog back!"

"Take it easy, lady!" Ed got off the stool. Quill kept
her grip on his hair.

John rose and gently peeled her fingers away. "I was
just about to go to work on getting Max back, Quill.
Why don't we make the call from your office?"

He drew her around the bar and out into the hall,
which led to her office and the lobby out front. She
shook her hand free of his and leaned against the wall.
"Sorry," she said after a moment.

"It's been a long day." John stood quietly, his arms
folded.

Quill looked at him sheepishly. "Guess I flipped my
cork. But, John, they can't put my dog down."

"Well, they can. But they won't do it without a court
order, and that will take a few days. I'll give Flick
Peterson a call right now. Just keep cool, buddy."

Quill followed him to the office, her palms sweaty
and her heart beat erratic. She bit her thumb nervously
during John's call to the dog warden, which consisted
mainly of "Right. Okay. I'll check." He hung up, and
before he could say anything, she said, "I've got a
plan."

"We don't need a plan."

"Yes, we do."

"Why do I think it involves kidnapping your dog
and sending him to Great-Aunt Matilda?"

Quill laughed a little. "Not Great-Aunt Matilda. But

Meg and I *do* have a Cousin Madeline, although she's not a blood relation, she's a cousin by choice, and she does love dogs. So I'm not going to flip out over this, John. If worse comes to worst, I'll just take Max to her."

"Where does Madeline live?"

"San Diego."

John's expression didn't change. "I've got a contingency plan. It doesn't involve turning Max into a fugitive. Want to hear it?"

"Sure."

"We wait and find out what happened. We don't shoot from the hip."

"I'd like to shoot those scriptwriters *in* the hip," Quill muttered. "Or any other handy spot."

John glanced at the clock on her desk. "It's after seven. Go into the kitchen and get something to eat."

"I'm going to get Max out of the slam, John." She brushed her hair back with both hands, straightened her shoulders, and took three determined strides down the hall before she stopped and turned back. "Where is the pound?"

"Out on Route 15. In Flick Peterson's backyard."

"Flick Peterson's backyard? That place is a dump! The front yard's filled with dead appliances and rusty bedsprings. God knows what the backyard's like!"

"Flick's the animal control officer," John said patiently.

Quill braced herself for an argument. "Max can't stay there, John. I won't leave him there overnight. I'll dognap him if I have to."

"We don't have much choice, Quill. But we can

probably bring him some food. Why don't we do that?"

"Why don't I find those bozo scriptwriters and give them a piece of my mind!" Quill said indignantly. "That poor dog never hurt anyone in his whole life!"

One of John's eyebrows went up, just a little. "You really think Flick's fed Max? My guess is, since he wasn't prepared for another animal, he'll wait until morning to feed him."

"I know what you're doing, John," she said ominously.

"And?"

"And you're right." She waved her arms. "I can't fight the whole system. I won't try and fight the system. But those scriptwriters are going to be sorry they did this! I'll find out who murdered Strickland if it's the last thing I do! That will get Max out of the doghouse, won't it?"

"If it doesn't put us in it," he said. "Visit your dog, Quill. We'll sort this out later, when the facts are all in."

CHAPTER 5

"Dangerous dog," Flick Peterson said. He used his tongue to flick the toothpick in his mouth from the right side to the left. Then he scratched under his armpit. Somewhere in the distance, a dog howled dolefully. Quill knew that howl.

Quill glared at him. "Max is not a dangerous dog." She swept her gaze around Flick's living room cum office. Flick was a collector. Old newspapers lay in waist-high stacks in the corners. Green plastic garbage bags of indeterminate stuff were shoved in a pile against one wall. An assortment of gutted televisions, fiberboard end tables, and boxes of glass jars littered the dusty wood floor. "But I'm going to get pretty dangerous if you don't let me see him!"

Max howled again.

Flick grinned and winked at John. "Minit I seen that

red hair, I shoulda known she was a spunky one."

Quill's eyes narrowed. She drew in a deep breath. Flick held one hand up in a placating way. He was deeply, cheerfully grimy in a dark blue cotton work shirt and pants. "Now don't get your knickers in a twist, Mrs. Quillam."

"It's Miss. And it's Quilliam. With an *i*."

"Callin' this here dog a dangerous dog ain't up to me. Nosir, it's up to the state of New York. Section 121 of the Agricultural and Marketing Code. We call it the Aggie-Maggie code. Cute, huh? Anyhow, what it says is, any dog what bites—"

"Max didn't bite anybody!"

"Well, no, I can't say that anyone's accused him of bitin'. And I met a lot of bitin' dogs in my time, and I would have to say in a court of law that that there dog's a pretty friendly dog, and not one of what you call your chronic biters—"

"Mr. Peterson . . ."

"—but I can't say, Mrs. Quillam, that that there dog isn't a murderer. Nosir. I can't say that. That, ma'am, is for a judge to decide." He flicked the toothpick to the other side of his mouth.

Quill subsided in defeat. "Can I at least see him?"

"Well, now, I don't usually allow that. Upsets the animal something fierce."

Quill held up the plastic bag of kibbles she'd brought. "He hasn't had his dinner yet, Mr. Peterson." Max's howls changed in depth and intensity. "And he'll stop that howling if he eats."

Flick bit the toothpick. "He howl like that at home?"

"Well, no. That is to say, just when he's hungry."

"A-huh." Flick got to his feet with a groan and fished a large bunch of keys from his pocket. "Howlers," he informed them as he led the way through his indescribably filthy kitchen and out the screen door. "Now, your howler ain't generally a biter."

The backyard was a bit of a shock. The grass was clipped short, and there wasn't a weed in sight. A neat row of chain-link cages formed a U around the perimeter. Each cage held a good six inches of clean wood shavings, a stainless-steel bowl of water, and an animal.

Max stopped howling the minute John and Quill stepped into the yard, and began to bark. This set off a chorus of yips, howls, barks, mews, and growls from the other creatures. Quill resisted the impulse to stick her fingers in her ears.

"Hush now," Flick said. Max was in the center cage at the back of the yard. Quill and John followed Flick. He paused briefly at each cage as he headed toward Max, dispensing what looked like fried liver bits (to a raccoon, a dog fox, and a Labrador retriever) and carrots (to a rabbit and a miniature horse).

Max flung himself against the wire cage. Quill knelt in front of it.

"Hang on a bit, Maxie," Flick said. "You're a lucky dog, you howler, you. You got a pretty lady come see you." He fumbled with the lock to the cage door and edged the door back. Max stuck his head anxiously through the small opening. "Here now," Flick said. He took Max's collar and, with surprisingly gentle fingers, smoothed the dog's floppy ears around his head. "You are an *ugly* one!" he said admiringly. "Here you go. Here's your ma."

Quill realized her mouth was open. She closed it. "Thank you, Mr. Peterson," she said. Then, noting Max's neatly brushed coat and clean paws, "You've been taking wonderful care of him."

Max jumped up, placed a forepaw on either shoulder, and frantically licked her face.

"Down, Max," she said. She grabbed his paws with both hands and shoved back. Max, panting heavily, looked at her beseechingly. "Oh, dear. You've got something in your back teeth. Mr. Peterson?"

"Huh! Thought I got all of that out." The dog warden took Max's muzzle in one hand and poked his finger quickly down the dog's throat. Max coughed and dropped to all four paws. Quill knelt down and emptied the paper bag of kibbles on the ground.

"Were you eating grass, you foolish dog?" she asked him.

"Not grass," Flick said. "Somebody's ass, more like." He took a plastic evidence bag from his back pocket and delicately inserted his hand in it. "Shirt cloth." He held the bag up for Quill's inspection. "Blue denim cloth. It's a kind a cotton," he explained kindly. "Comes from a man's shirt, most like."

Quill cleared her throat. "You found more of this cloth in his jaws?"

"Well now. That I did. Boys that brung him in said they brung him straight from the scene of the crime. Staties brought the dog in," Flick continued. "Had to catch him with the pole collar. Dog wouldn't let no one near him." He scratched under the other armpit and gazed thoughtfully at the raccoon in the next cage over, which was hissing at Max. "Max didn't mind me pettin' him, though. It's when I found them other pieces. Had to turn the first bit of cloth over to them right away. It's evidence, like."

"Don't you find it suspicious that Flick conveniently found another shred of shirt while we just happened to be there to witness it?" Quill bent forward and tucked the empty kibble bag in the glove compartment of the car. She'd have to remember to bring more to Max tomorrow.

John kept his eyes on the road, but she saw a muscle in his jaw twitch. "Yes."

"And the only person in a denim shirt is Mort Carmody. Who supposedly was drunk in his room at the relevant times. And whose testimony, so to speak, put Max in the slam. We have a suspect, John."

"We don't have a murder, yet. Shouldn't we wait for the autopsy?"

"Okay, okay!" She slumped back in the seat. "What do we do now? Will Howie Murchison represent Max? Will there be a trial?"

"Howie's town justice," John said. "And we're looking at a violation, Quill. It's not even a misdemeanor. The town justice rules on violations. But I guess we can present a defense."

"Character witnesses," Quill said. "We can get character witnesses."

"Harland Peterson, for example?" John said with a slight smile. Max had made significant inroads on Harland's chicken population.

"Esther West?"

"Ditto for Esther's Dumpster in back of the shop on Main Street."

"Marge Schmidt, perhaps? Or maybe Miriam Doncaster?"

John shook his head.

"The veterinarian, then," Quill said, remembering Miriam's outraged phone call after the episode of Max and the drying laundry. "He can swear to the fact that Max isn't vicious."

John didn't reply to this. Which was just as well, since the local vet had refused to treat the dog anymore after Max shoved over the drug cabinet and destroyed several hundred dollars' worth of Ace Promazine, Betadyne, and Butazoladin. Twice.

"He hasn't done anything to the vet in Syracuse," Quill said after a moment. "And there's tons of canine experts at the Cornell Veterinary School. We could hire them to come in and defend Max."

"Max hasn't been to the vet in Syracuse yet," John said. "And what would experts from Cornell have to say about a—let's be charitable and call him a crossbreed. Experts can testify generally about propensities in breeds, Quill. But not about a—"

"Don't call him a mutt." Quill folded her arms and stared out the window. John turned smoothly into the drive leading up the hill to the Inn. The long day was drawing to a close. Orange and yellow streaked the western sky, framing the sprawling old building in brilliant color. A departing state trooper's car passed them on the left. John pulled into the circular drive and came to a stop in front of the oak door. He touched her arm.

"I'll put the car away. I want you to get something to eat and then turn in. It's been a tough day."

Quill smiled at him. "Thanks for coming with me."

"We'll manage through this, Quill." He shifted slightly in the seat, and his scent came to Quill, a faint spicy odor of the outdoors.

She withdrew. She could feel it, and she knew he felt it, too, although neither of them moved. She said nothing, but got out of the car and went into the foyer.

To her surprise, Dina was sitting behind the reception desk. Quill greeted her with a wave. "Thought you'd be home by now."

Dina shook her head and yawned. "Nope. Doreen had to go home to give Stoke the scoop on the murder, Meg and Andy went off to Syracuse for dinner because Meg said she was too rattled to cook, and nobody knew where you and John were, so I stuck around to wait for the new guest."

Quill frowned. "What new guest? We're not open yet, except for those guys from L.A."

"This is another guy from L.A. Mr. Strickland's lawyer. I guess Benny Gilpin called him as soon as they found the corpse and he hopped on the next plane to the East Coast."

Quill looked at her watch. "It's eight-thirty. When's he due?"

"Eleven o'clock. I don't mind staying late, Quill, honestly." She tapped her laptop. "I'm working on the thesis, and I'm on-line to the Cornell Library, so I might as well do it here rather than at the dorm."

"You'd better stay over, then. There must be a room that's set up."

"Two, as a matter of fact. One for me, and one for this lawyer." Dina rubbed her nose, then glanced sideways at Quill. "Where were you and John?"

"I went to try and get Max out of dog jail. No soap."

"Poor Max," Dina said, although to Quill's mind, she didn't sound all that regretful. "Is he okay?"

"He's fine. The dog warden is really weird, but he seems to like animals."

"Good. Good," Dina said thoughtfully.

"Good what?" Quill demanded. "Is there anything else wrong?"

"I thought maybe you and John might be talking to Howie."

"Max needs character witnesses," Quill said. "Not a lawyer. Although if he does, I'll get one."

"A lawyer for Max? I was thinking that we'd need a lawyer for us."

Quill was pretty sure that she didn't want to know what was coming next. "For us?" she said hollowly. "You don't mean . . ."

Dina nodded. "You have to expect it these days. The L.A. lawyer's secretary? When she called to make the reservations? She said to label the bills with a case file number, which she gave me, and *Estate of Neil Strickland* v. *Quilliam et al.*"

Quill put both hands on top of her head and pulled her hair as hard as she could. "Fine," she said shortly. "Just *fine!*"

There was a brief silence.

"Can I do anything?" Dina asked timidly. "Can I get you something to eat?"

"Why does everyone want to feed me? I'm going up

to my room," Quill said with as much dignity as she could muster, "and I am going to take a hot bath and drink a martini."

"You don't drink martinis."

"I'm starting a career of drinking martinis." Quill slung her purse over her shoulder and started to go upstairs. She glanced through the archway to the dining room, a habit hard to break after nine years of managing the Inn. The tables were empty, of course; they wouldn't officially open until Labor Day. She'd been looking forward to seeing the dining room filled with the quiet chatter of satisfied guests, scenting the garlicky butter smell of escargots Quilliam, hearing the unmistakable *pop* as a good bottle of red wine was opened.

And now someone else wanted to take the Inn away from them.

She straightened her back and marched upstairs. She was going to see, hear, and smell all those future customers no matter what happened.

She opened the door to her rooms with a hearty shove. The last bit of the sunset flared at the French windows on the far side of her living room. At first, she didn't see him sitting in the reading chair.

"Myles!"

"Sorry. I didn't mean to startle you." He had a notebook computer in his lap. He closed it and stood up. She couldn't see his face against the color flooding the room. "I was just reviewing some of the statements Davey took at the scene. I was planning on waiting downstairs, but the tavern bar's full of scriptwriters and Dina's in the foyer."

"And she talks and talks and talks. Well," Quill said uncertainly. She snapped on the lights. The last of the sunset faded. Myles looked tired in the lamplight. Deep circles shadowed his eyes. "As a matter of fact, I was going to give you a call. Have you had anything to eat yet?"

"I'm fine," he said.

"Well, I'm not. I'm starving. I haven't had a thing since lunch." Aware that she was chattering, she moved brightly into her kitchen and opened the refrigerator drawer under the counter. "What about an omelette?"

"You go ahead."

"I've a bit of Gruyère, too. And a little brioche." She broke five eggs into a stainless-steel bowl and took out the whisk.

Myles hesitated. This was so uncharacteristic that Quill whisked too hard and splashed half of the egg mixture into the sink. She dumped the bowl out and started all over again. "Glass of wine?" she asked.

"Fine." Myles settled onto one of the stools at the kitchen counter. Quill felt some of the tension leave her shoulders. She poured them both a glass of Vouvray then turned the gas flame on under the omelette pan. "So have you found out who did it?" She kept her voice light.

"Andy won't be sure until he gets the autopsy report. But it looks as if Strickland hit his head on a flagstone."

"Or someone hit him with it."

"Or someone hit him with it," Myles agreed. "We found a piece with what looks like blood and hair. The edge is quite sharp. He may have rolled quite a way down. There was a lot of damage to the face and hands."

Quill tipped the eggs into the pan and began to grate the cheese. "So what do you think, Myles? If ever a guy was ripe for murder, Strickland was. I mean, I only met him for those few seconds, but, ugh!"

"We'll see. The scriptwriters are booked for the next two weeks, aren't they? I've asked them to stay at least that amount of time."

"All I have to say is, Max didn't do it. And I'm glad that you're on the case, Myles. You always get it right."

"That's why I've dropped by." Again that odd tentativeness.

Quill split the omelette in half, put it on two plates, and served both of them. "You're going away," she said. She sat next to him. She didn't feel anything at all, she thought. Not a thing. She had a strong impulse to scream. What did she want? Whom did she want? Why should she feel anything? She didn't love Myles anymore—did she? She looked at him as if he were sitting for a portrait, trying to see past the strong face and the broad shoulders to the man beneath. What if he had a Bronx accent? What if he were six inches shorter and didn't have a broad, heavily muscled, hairy chest?

"Well, yes, Quill. I told you about the forensics convention in Seattle weeks ago."

"Oh." A little deflated, she put a forkful of hot omelette in her mouth and spit it out hastily. "Yes, you did. You're the guest speaker."

"They can't replace me on such short notice."

"So who's going to take over the investigation?" Her eyes widened. "Not that jerk from the state troopers' barracks. Not Harris!"

"Harris is a perfectly capable officer." Myles ate his eggs. Quill, annoyed, thought that he was amused.

"He doesn't like me," she said. "Or Meg."

"He doesn't care for amateurs mixing up in official investigations," Myles said dryly. "If you and Meg didn't consider yourselves this generation's answer to Nero Wolfe, you'd get along fine with Harris."

"Mother Teresa couldn't get along with Harris," Quill said. "And she's dead. What about Max? What about the Inn? Dina just told me—"

"Everett Bland's coming in from L.A. to file a civil action," Myles said. "I know. But not too much can happen in a week, Quill."

Quill flung her hands wildly over her head. "Oh, I don't know. We bombed Iraq into surrender in a week. Plays on Broadway have bombed in three days. Aaagh, Myles! What if they find Max guilty and they shoot him?"

"If Max scared Strickland over the edge of the Gorge, which is possible, Quill, at most you'll have to keep the dog tied up. Which might not be such a bad thing. Well." He slid off the stool. "That's it. I came by to say good-bye. I'll leave the hotel number with Davey, if you need to get in touch."

"You didn't drink your wine," she said.

"Maybe next time." He bent over her, his face expressionless. He drew one finger across her lips.

Then he was gone.

Quill washed the plates and the wineglasses and walked restlessly around her apartment. During Marge's brief tenure, she'd rented Quill's rooms as a suite; even though her own furniture was moved back in, the place still had the scent of rented rooms.

"My *life* has the scent of rented rooms," Quill said aloud. She circled the room once more. Sherri's bag of herbal remedies sat accusingly on her sideboard. She looked at her watch: nine forty-five. A little late to go down to Sherri's, but she could use the walk.

The moon was at the half, and the air was a delight. The night swam with the scents of summer; cut grass, the fragrance of Oriental lilies, a whiff of lavender. The light was on in John's carriage house. Her steps faltered a little as she walked past.

Did she need *any* men in her life?

Quill walked briskly down the curving driveway to Main Street. Friday night, and she could hear the music from the Croh Bar half a mile away. The place would be jammed with people, dating people, couples . . .

Men were such a *pain,* she thought crossly. She was going to take vows and become a nun. That'd show everyone.

The lights were on in Sherri's gym. A red minivan was parked in the street in front of the door, in back of Sherri's little Volkswagen. The door itself was partly open. Quill tapped cheerfully and stepped in, "Sherri? It's Sarah Quilliam." She could just see Sherri in the back of the gym. Her arms were wrapped around a tall guy in a passionate embrace. Her T-shirt was on the floor. Quill's face flamed in embarrassment. She shut the door hastily and retreated into the street. She walked back home furious with herself, with Myles, with John, with the whole human race. She went back upstairs to her rooms, flung the bag into a corner, and kicked at the floor pillows.

The knock at her door made her jump. Annoyed at the relief that washed through her—couldn't she stand to be alone for a minute?—she shouted a grouchy "come in."

"I saw Myles leave a while ago," Meg said as she walked in the door. "Did you two get things straightened out?"

"No." Quill eyed her sister.

Meg made a face, wrinkling her nose and sticking out her tongue. She was wearing a paint-spattered pair of old shorts, a baggy T-shirt, and no shoes. She looked about six years old.

"Did you go to Syracuse like that?"

"I decided not to go to Syracuse." She walked past Quill into the living room and settled on the couch.

Quill followed her a little reluctantly, then sat down in the leather Eames chair facing her. She didn't feel like more confrontation. Even though she had failed miserably to confront Myles. Except that it felt as if she'd been through a confrontation. She dug her hands in her hair and pulled hard.

Meg tugged at her lower lip. "Do you know what you want?"

"Both of them. Neither of them. I don't know."

"If you don't know, Quill, maybe you shouldn't even try to make a decision. Maybe you just haven't met the right person yet."

"Meg—how many guys have you slept with?"

Meg opened her mouth, then closed it. "Hmm," she said in a guarded way.

"Hmm is not an answer."

"Shut up. I'm counting." Her eyes took on a faraway look. Her lips moved slightly. She grinned suddenly. "Huh! What about you? How many guys have you slept with?"

"Three," Quill replied promptly. "Phillip from high school, Dan, and Myles."

"One ex-husband and two lovers?" Meg's eyebrows rose in a superior way. "That's all?"

"What do you mean that's all? As far as I know, you haven't dated anyone but Andrew since we moved here nine years ago. And before that, there was Simon, and before that . . . what? Who?"

Meg waved her hand airily. "A few. A few. Sex is like food, Quill. You have to have some basis for comparison. Not hundreds and hundreds, of course," she added hastily. "But a few more than three. And one of those with Phillip, the captain of the basketball team in high school? Oho! Well, there you are. Sleep with John and find out."

"I beg your pardon?" Quill said stiffly.

"You don't really know a guy until you've been to bed with him," Meg said. "And if you don't know, find out."

"But—"

"Well, yeah. If you sleep with John, that means your relationship with Myles is over. Kaput. Finito. So yes, you do have to make that decision right now. Although," Meg added thoughtfully. "Myles is a pretty good guy. He might forgive you. But, Quillie, I don't think you could forgive yourself." She bounced up. "Now that I've accomplished that most satisfying of activities—"

"Which most satisfying of activities? Driving me crazy?"

"Astonishing my older sister . . . Hey, I'm out of here. It's late. Look, you know that the Chamber meeting is tomorrow morning?"

"Yes, um," Quill concentrated. Her management responsibilities seemed very far away. "Right. Brunch for thirty."

"You don't have to worry about it. Bjarne is handling it. Adela Henry just called. She made reservations for five more. That means Bjarne's got to order more fruit and bake two more pounds of brioche in the morning. I left him a note in the kitchen, but I want you to make sure that he sees it. Okay?"

"You're not going to be here at all tomorrow?"

"I'm at La Strazza tomorrow."

"But it's Saturday!"

Meg's lower lip jutted out. "They just called, okay? Anatole Supinsky walked out of the kitchen this afternoon. For good, they think."

"Anatole walks out of the kitchen six times a week!"

"This time he got on a plane to Budapest. And they're pretty sure that the *Times* food critic is going to be there tomorrow night, and I'm sorry, Quill, but I can't afford to pass this chance up. The *Times* hasn't reviewed me for years. And we want the Inn to keep its stars, don't we?"

"You aren't going to be here, so what does it matter?"

"Of course I'm going to be here. I'm not going to just leave you flat, Quill."

"What about the junk food Horvath wants?"

"No."

"What if he puts in a pool and we have a pool bar?"

"Maybe. But I'm not just going to walk out on you. We have a deal."

"It sure as hell sounded like you were going today!"

"I was mad at you today. And I was feeling guilty, okay? You know me, I lose my temper and I say things I don't mean, and for God's sake, Quill, you aren't going to try and make me stay here just to cook a brunch for the flippin' Chamber of Commerce? They put ketchup on my *pâté*!" Meg's nostrils flared, her face turned pink, and her eyes bugged out.

Quill reached over and grabbed her arm. *"Stop!"* she said firmly. "Of course I don't mind if you cook at La Strazza tomorrow."

"I'll commute home!" Meg roared. "Except I'll be commuting from New York to here, rather than the other way around. That's all that's going to change!"

"Fine," Quill said tartly. "Fine. Except that you might not have anything to commute to, Meg."

"What do you mean?"

"Strickland's lawyer is flying in to sue us."

"Who told you that?"

"Dina."

"Oh." Meg's eyes narrowed. "Why?"

"For not controlling Max, I guess. You know people can sue anyone over anything these days."

"Hmm. What does Howie say?"

"Haven't talked to him yet. And besides, he may

have to recuse himself because he's the town justice and he'll hear Max's case when it comes up. If Howie has to decide whether Max is a dangerous dog, I don't think he can represent us in a lawsuit where we have to prove Max isn't a dangerous dog."

"Max? Dangerous? That dog's an idiot, but he's not lethal."

"Well, our wonderful judicial system is going to try and prove he is," Quill said. "Strickland's lawyer's going to try to prove it, too, I think. I mean, it can only help their case against us if Max is put down for killing Neil Strickland."

"Wow." Meg scratched a mosquito bite on her ankle with a thoughtful expression. "And I don't suppose that the Finnish government is going to be too happy about a lawsuit."

"No," Quill said glumly.

"Maybe we can keep it from Horvath."

"And maybe pigs can fly."

"But we've already been through discovery, Quill. I mean, Horvath knows everything about our financials already—"

"Meg!"

"You're right, you're right. Poor Quillie. I can't believe we're in a huge mess already. And the Inn isn't open yet!"

"We'll get through this," Quill said firmly. "We've been through worse."

"Does this mean you and I are going to try and find out who killed Strickland?"

Quill closed her eyes. "All of a sudden we're back in business? Sisters forever? I've been mooching around all day long feeling like a heel and a jerk because I drove my own sister out of my life! I mean, I'm having the worst day of my life, the *worst*—"

"It's not the worst," Meg said knowledgeably. "Wasn't the day of your divorce worse?"

"Was my dog dead when I got divorced! Was I about to lose the roof over my head because of a sleazy lawyer!"

"Your dog's not dead." Meg looked a little doubtful. "Not yet, anyway."

"I'm going to hit you with a large stick. I'm going to brain you with a . . ." Quill opened her eyes and looked wildly around. Three fat pillows were stacked on the floor near the French doors. She grabbed the top one (scarlet Thai silk) and pitched it. Meg ducked with a shriek, clutched the pillow by one corner, and whacked Quill over the head. Quill retaliated with the second pillow (sage-green velveteen).

Both of them stopped thumping each other when Dina tapped at the door, walked in, and shouted, "Guys? *Guys!*" She glared at them, her arms folded over her stomach.

"What?" Meg demanded. She tucked in her T-shirt with a grin. Quill stacked the pillows on the floor. "Is there another murder?" Meg asked sunnily.

"There's about to be," Dina said grimly. "This guy from L.A. has some kind of order to close the Inn down." She scowled ferociously, an incongruous expression for someone as cheerfully pretty as Dina. "And if you don't shoot him, I'm going to."

CHAPTER 6

Everett Bland sat at ease on the sagging leather couch in front of the cobblestone fireplace. He had sunglasses on. He was tanned, fit, and wore expensively cut, well-worn jeans and a slouchy sort of blue sport coat over a white shirt open at the neck. Quill thought he was in his early forties, despite the carefully barbered gray hair. He got to his feet as Meg, Quill, and Dina clattered down the stairs. When he faced them, Quill realized he was in his late fifties, perhaps even older. There was no disguising how skin thinned as you aged—no matter how much collagen was pumped under your eyes and into your upper lip.

Bland didn't smile. "Which one of you is Sarah Quilliam?"

"I am." Quill extended her hand.

Bland took it, squeezed hard, and released it as if

dropping a dead fish. "You have a wonderful old building here."

"Thank you," Quill said. "We love it very much. Dina tells me you're trying to close us down."

He gave her a close-lipped smile. "I have an order, yes. From a judge in Los Angeles, which I'm sure you know isn't valid here in New York."

Quill controlled her impatience. "Then what's this all about?"

Bland wandered to the cobblestone mantel and ran his thumb over the creamy stones. "When was this place built?"

"The original building was put up in the late 1600s. It was a way station for trappers headed on up to Canada. There's an old stone smokehouse out back that dates from that time. The Inn as you see it now was constructed over a period of two hundred years. The fireplace dates from the Revolutionary War. The copper roof was put on when the Inn was a residence during the Civil War."

"Who lived here?"

"General C. C. Hemlock," Meg said impatiently. "Why do you care?"

"Just getting an idea of its value on the open market." He took off his sunglasses and tucked them into his shirt pocket. "And to answer your question, the order to cease business is a precaution. I'll take it in to a local judge if I need to." He took a document folded lengthwise from his coat pocket. "You understand."

"I do not," Meg said tartly.

He shrugged. "Do you have representation, Miss . . . ?"

"Quilliam," Meg said. Her cheeks were flushed. "And if by 'representation' you mean do we have a lawyer, everybody has a lawyer, Mr. Bland. And the reason everybody has a lawyer is because everyone *else* has a lawyer."

Everett Bland was clearly used to hearing verbal potshots about lawyers. He continued, in an unperturbed way, "Then if the lovely redhead here is Sarah Quilliam, you must be Meg. I've heard about your skills in the kitchen. I'm looking forward to eating here."

"You can look forward to McDonald's," Meg snapped. "And to a room at the Holiday Inn."

"Ah-ah-ah?" He shook his head and waved the document gently in front of her face. "As I said. A precaution. I'll be staying here. It will be easier to keep tabs on what's going on."

"And to find out how much you can gouge out of us, I suppose."

"I have to represent the interest of my client's estate, of course. And the best way to do that is to be where the action is, naturally." He drifted toward the reception desk. "Now, this is a fine old piece. Did this belong to—whom did you say lived here? General Hemlock?"

"We didn't say," Quill intervened. Meg was fully capable of grabbing the tongs from the fireplace and whacking Bland over his head. "And you're not precisely welcome here, Mr. Bland, but we do have a room for you. All we ask is a little discretion. Publicity about the terrible accident to Mr. Strickland can't be good for any of us."

"Perhaps. Perhaps not. You can trust in my discretion. With all due modesty, I haven't achieved my current position as lawyer to the stars without a sufficiency of discretion."

Quill looked at Meg. Meg mouthed "Horvath" and scowled horribly. Quill grimaced. She wondered if she could keep Bland's plans from Horvath. Or even if she should try. Bland's suitcase rested next to the leather couch. He nudged it meaningfully with the toe of his alligator loafer. "Do we have a room for Mr. Bland, Dina?" Quill asked.

"Doreen set up Suite Three," Dina said.

Quill thought about this. Doreen didn't subscribe to the Quilliam notions of hospitality, in particular the third rule of innkeeping (don't whack unwelcome guests with the wet mop). She was more than capable of putting something slimy in Mr. Bland's sheets, or booby-trapping the toilet. Did Quill want a litigious lawyer in Suite Three?

"And you're sleeping where?"

"Two-seventeen," Dina said suspiciously. She'd been with them long enough to know Doreen's propensities. Actually, anyone who worked for the Inn for more than two days discovered Doreen's propensities for avenging slights and annoyances.

"That room's the one with the nice view of the Falls," Quill said cheerfully. "I think you'll be very happy in there, Mr. Bland. The view is remarkable."

"The suite sounds fine. I have a lot of work with me. I'll need the space."

"The suite's right over the kitchen," Quill said.

"Two-ten's over the kitchen," Dina said firmly, "and Mr. Schwartz is in there, and besides, no one has ever complained about it!"

Quill's voice rose over Dina's. "Two-seventeen gets sort of garlicky in the afternoon, Mr. Bland. And the sous-chef whistles a theme from *Finlandia* over and over again when he's working."

"I don't want the suite!" Dina wailed. "I'll have to check for slugs in the sheets!"

Mr. Bland's California cool slipped a little. "Well . . . ah. Two-seventeen, you said?"

"Dina, would you show Mr. Bland to his room?"

There was a shuffle-slam at the front door. Quill turned in surprise. It was well after eleven-thirty. Horvath Kierkegaard closed the door behind him and raised his hand in cheerful salute. "My dear Miss Quilliam! And the so lovely Miss Meg. And . . . you." He looked a little nervously at Dina.

"Hey, Mr. Kierkegaard," she said.

"Hey," he said. "That is correct? Just 'Hey'?"

"That is correct."

"How are you, Miss Muir?"

"Fine. I'll be a lot finer if you keep your hands off my butt."

"Of course, of course!" Horvath advanced cautiously. He smelled strongly of beer and french fries. "I have been to Syracuse," he said. His round face beamed. "There is a festival there!"

"The state fair," Quill said. "I'd forgotten about it."

"The food!" Horvath said dreamily. "The potatoes, the cotton candy. The funny cakes! It is bliss."

"*Funnel* cakes," Meg said. "Glad you enjoyed yourself."

"And only you, Horvath, could come to one of the best chefs in America and sneak off for junk food," Everett Bland said. He smiled. *Really* smiled, not the tight-lipped smirk he'd given Quill and Meg a few moments before. "How are you, Kierkegaard? Keeping your hand in up here?"

"It is not! It is not my old friend Everett Bland!" Horvath bounced forward past Quill and grasped both of Bland's hands. He wriggled like a delighted puppy.

Meg, who was standing to Bland's right, looked curiously from one to the other. "You know each other?"

"But of course!" Horvath said warily. "I have spent many happy hours in Los Angeles."

"At the Taco Bell, mostly," Bland said. "So you're here as well, Horvath. Checking out the countryside, I suppose?"

They exchanged a knowing glance. Quill raised her eyebrows at Meg, who shrugged "beats me."

Horvath bounced gently on his toes. "Oh yes. Oh yes. Do not tell me. Let me guess. You are interested in buying this marvelous old Inn as well."

"As well as what?" Dina demanded. "Are you buying something else?"

Horvath looked at Quill. To a casual viewer, he seemed happy. Quill noticed the smile didn't reach his eyes, and that his left hand played nervously with the change in his trouser pocket. "You know, our friend Mr. Bland is a real estate—what is the English word? Maven. Without peer."

"The word's Yiddish," Dina said in rather a didactic

way. "And I thought you were Mr. Strickland's attorney, Mr. Bland."

Bland tucked the order to close into his jacket pocket. "I like to diversify. Only way to true wealth, eh, Horvath?"

"The only way, indeed." Horvath shook his head to signal admiration. "And you, my old friend, have good lessons to teach. How I will learn from my experience in America!"

Quill had seen part of a bullfight one summer in Spain (she left the arena when it got bloody); the stance of the two men reminded her of the way bull and matador had regarded one another. Horvath was the bull, wary and ready to charge; Bland, the matador.

"So you know each other," she said brightly.

"We've established that," Meg said. "The question is, why do you know each other? And was it through Mr. Strickland?"

"Very sorry to hear of his passing," Horvath said. "The news was on the car radio. And the doggie is where? Locked up, I presume?"

"For the moment," Quill said. "But he didn't attack anyone. Well, not after the first time."

"Did you know Mr. Strickland?" Meg persisted.

"In an informal way, yes, I did," Horvath replied. "I was sorry not to have met him before his demise. Now. I am afraid I must bid you all good night. I have an early date. I will see you in the morning, Quill? At the gym?"

"At the gym?" Quill said, astonished. "You're joining the class?"

"Oh yes. I am not getting enough exercise at all.

One drives everywhere here. And the first session is free, isn't it?" He took a "Get Buff!" flyer. "See? There is a paragraph that states there is an eight-o'clock-in-the-morning aerobics class, absolutely free for first-timers. I am a first-timer. It is called"—he frowned at the copy—"Kick-Start. That is an American expression, is it not?" He offered the flyer to Bland, who shook his head. "Not for me. I run in the mornings."

"I thought it was called Practical Aerobics," Meg said. "That's what Marge told me, anyhow."

"Marge?" Everett Bland said, "Marge Schmidt? Is she in the exercise class?"

"It's Shakin' with Sherri," Dina said. "She told me Inn employees get a ten-percent discount. On the other hand, Adela Henry said it's named Sensuous Seniors. Maybe there's more than one."

"Maybe she changes the name to suit the sucker," Meg suggested cynically.

"Another coup for the world greatest detective!" Dina said. "That's it!"

Quill felt hopelessly out of it. "She told me it was called 'Get With It.' "

Meg patted her arm. "Can't *wait* to see your pecs."

"Detective?" Bland's eyebrows rose.

"Actually, both of them are," Dina said proudly. "Although I think Meg's got the edge."

"No, she doesn't," Quill said. "I've discovered the important clue in every single case we've had."

"Says you!" Meg said.

"Says you!" Quill riposted.

They laughed immoderately.

Bland cleared his throat meaningfully and nudged

his suitcase again. Dina muttered, "Jeez!" but picked it up and preceded the lawyer up the stairs.

Horvath stared after him, then said good night and trudged up after them.

Quill went thoughtfully to bed.

CHAPTER 7

Ten minutes into Sherri Kerri's eight-o'clock-in-the-morning class, Get Fit (or maybe it *was* Sensuous Seniors; she didn't know and didn't care) Quill wanted her money back. She hated it. It was worse than a root canal and gum surgery at the same time. She'd *rather* have root canal and gum surgery at the same time than flail in unison with her fellows.

The gym floor was jammed with huffing, puffing, sweating women and one cheerful Finn. They were doing step aerobics. Step aerobics involved climbing off and on a little bench while every other body part did something else to truly awful music.

Horvath ran nimbly up and down, lunged to the left like a fencer, lunged to the right like a tennis player, and didn't trip over his feet once. All the while he chatted up Marge Schmidt. Marge trotted up, trotted down, lunged left and right like a boxer, and seemed to be having a fine old time, too.

Esther West was enthusiastic and coordinated, Miriam Doncaster earnest and coordinated, and Adela Henry was *good,* as graceful as an Olympian.

"Step *up*!" Sherri shouted. "Step down!"

Quill stepped up and fell off.

"And *up*!"

She tried again.

"And *down*! Quill?"

"I *am* down," Quill said crossly. She picked herself up and brushed her knees.

"Keep it up, ladies! Re-peat! Re-peat! Step *up* and . . . Quill?"

"I'm going to try the treadmill!"

"What?" Sherri wasn't even breaking a sweat. Quill pointed at the treadmill. Sherri nodded vigorously. Quill wound her way through the smell of damp talcum powder, bleach (from the clean gym clothes), and sweaty socks. The treadmill loomed, a lifesaver.

Quill switched it on, and the LED screen promptly displayed a series of insolent questions.

WEIGHT?

She punched in her real actual weight, less five pounds.

FITNESS LEVEL?

She pressed "1," then enter.

SPEED OR TIME?

Quill thought about this.

?????

"Shut *up*," Quill whispered, then punched "time." Then, "15 minutes." She thought about her fitness level and pressed the reverse arrow key back to FITNESS LEVEL. After a hasty glance around the room to see if anyone was watching, she keyed "0."

SPEED? the LED asked.

"What the *heck*," Quill muttered, and punched the ten-miles-per-hour button, which was a snail's pace in the car.

START?

"Sure," Quill said, and punched the key.

All hell broke loose.

"You can't," Sherri explained a hectic five minutes later, "start out at level ten at ten miles an hour, Quill! No wonder you fell off the treadmill."

"I didn't fall off the treadmill."

"You fell off the treadmill and into poor Adela Henry!"

"The treadmill threw me across the room. And I'm sorry, Adela."

Adela nodded majestically. She feinted left and stepped to the music with ineffable grace. Quill wanted to scream.

Sherri taped another Band-Aid across Quill's shin, then checked the ice pack on her wrist with brisk competence. "Have a Power Drink and relax a little. On the house. The class has another ten minutes, then we'll *all* have a nice juice break."

Quill hitched herself up on a bar stool and sipped green gunk from a glass. The awful music ended with a blare. Everybody walked around the gym floor stretching and flexing with expressions of thoughtful absorption on their sweaty faces. Quill wondered what they were listening to. The screams of their overworked cardiovascular systems? The leaky-bellows whooshing of their lungs?

"You okay?" Marge plunked herself down on a stool.

"I feel like an idiot."

"I feel good," Marge said simply. "Thing is, Quill, you gotta start out slow. Can't set the treadmill at ten—"

"I know," Quill said.

"What're you drinking?"

"Some kind of power stuff. And I'm not drinking it exactly."

"That's Sherry's Power Drink. Gives you a good kick. Try it. All natural. Good for you."

Quill took a sip and made a face, which she regretted immediately, since she really did want Sherri Kerri's gym-and-health-food business to be successful. Just as long as she got her money back, and didn't have to go to war with gym equipment three times a week. "Tastes interesting," she managed. "Sort of like a broccoli-and-lima-bean milkshake." She handed it to Marge. "Would you like some?" She watched in morbid fascination as Marge downed the whole thing.

"Expensive stuff," Marge said. "So. How are you and Horvath getting along?"

"I don't know. He hasn't signed yet, Marge. I mean, we've gone through discovery, and we seem to agree about every point in the contract. Except for the food. He insists on, you know, popular foods."

"Junk food," Marge said bluntly. "Good profit margin in it, Quill, or there used to be."

"Oh, hang the profit margin."

"What's Meg say about it?"

"You know what Meg says about it. But why would Horvath offer to invest in the Inn, then stick at the very characteristic that makes it great?"

"Why indeed?" Marge said. "You might think about it."

"I have thought about it. And it doesn't make sense. I'll tell you what else doesn't make sense. You know Strickland's attorney's here." Marge nodded. Marge always knew what was going on in Hemlock Falls. "He and Horvath know each other. They both knew Strickland. And it's not just a 'met him in the airport' kind of an acquaintance. There's something funny going on."

"Oh, yeah?" Marge looked totally blank, which meant that her brain was racing like a computer. "What do you think?"

"I don't know what to think. But I'll tell you this— it's got to be connected to Neil Strickland's murder."

"Oh, yeah? So it's a murder?"

"Well, from the looks of it, yes," Quill said in a slightly professional tone. "An ax or a machete, is my guess." She ignored Marge's skeptical glance. "You just wait until the autopsy. Anyway, you know Max—"

"That damn dog."

"He didn't have anything to do with Strickland's death. But do you know what he had in his jaws?"

"Blood? Bone? Contents of my garbage cans?"

"Very funny. He had a piece of denim shirt. And the only person at the Inn in denim yesterday was Mort Carmody."

"The scriptwriter." Marge rubbed her chin in a meditative way. "Think we could get them all together? The scriptwriters, the Finn, and that lawyer? Get 'em talking about money. You'd be amazed at what'd come out when you get a bunch of men to talk about money. Especially if you give Mort a bottle of gin."

"You know about that?"

"All three of them closed the Croh Bar last night. You bet your Band-Aids I know about that."

Quill's eyes wandered to Horvath. He was standing at the ballet barre, stretching. "The scriptwriters are at the Tompkins County courthouse this morning," she said, "giving statements to the police. They made a late reservation for lunch. If you can come by the Inn at two, I think I'll be able to get them all in the same room and they won't have a clue that we're after information."

Marge burped slightly. "That'll be a trick."

Quill tried not to feel smug. "You'll see." She downed the last of the green gunk.

"You and Horvath here to see our new version of *Sneezer*?" Benny Gilpin pushed the remains of his potatoes *duchesse* around his plate. There were bits of cheese in his gray beard. Mort Carmody looked into his glass as if the secrets to the universe were there.

Eddie Schwartz showed all his teeth in a smile, "I think it's a good idea."

All three of them had returned from their interrogation with Captain Harris in subdued frames of mind. Meg's Asiago salad and tuna carpaccio had gone a long way toward cheering them up.

"Hey!" Eddie said confidently. "After all, if Neil hadn't gone on and on about meeting Horvath here in L.A., we wouldn't have gotten the idea in the first place."

"What idea?" Marge had her arms folded under her considerable bosom. She shifted impatiently from one foot to the other. She and Quill had waited in Quill's office until Kathleen Kiddermeister, the Inn's head waitress, had buzzed Quill to let them know the scriptwriters were about to leave the dining room. Quill swept Horvath from the flagstone terrace, where he was napping, and brought him into the dining room.

"Sneezer's a Finn now," Eddie said. He eyed Mort's cigarette. "Gimme one of those, Mort."

Marge took the cigarette Mort proffered, broke it in half, then removed the pack from Mort's shirt pocket. "You can't smoke in here. Now, what's this about a sneezing Finn?"

"It's a cartoon show," Quill said, "for kids. And I believe it's the very first time Finland has been so honored on American television, Horvath."

"This is very exciting," Horvath said politely. "I would very much like to see this."

"So we've set up the VCR in the conference room, and we're ready to roll. We have the demo tape you sent ahead, too."

Eddie nodded vigorously, "We should have thought of this, guys. You see—Horvath, is it? You might have a terrific opportunity here to invest in American TV with *The Sneezer Show!* This new pilot is a great tribute to Finland. Now that poor Neil—"

"God rest his soul!" Mort said suddenly, reducing them all to momentary silence.

Eddie waited a respectful moment. "Now that poor Neil has gone to his reward—"

"And we hope he gets exactly the reward he deserves," Benny muttered.

"We just may have a spot for a new investor." Eddie got up from the dining-room table and hunched over the shorter man. "I can't promise anything yet—"

"You can't promise anything at all," Everett Bland said. "Neil was the series producer, and until JoyMax makes a decision about who takes his spot, you three have no legal right to make those kinds of promises." He had obviously just come in from a jog; he wore black bicycle shorts, a loose T-shirt, and running shoes. A room towel was wound around his neck. He wiped his face with one edge and said to Quill, "I got your message. You want my legal opinion on this new series?"

"Excuse me?" Benny's tone was rudely intrusive. "Let's get to the decision-making process here. I'm senior scriptwriter. And JoyMax as good as promised me the producer's spot when and if old Neil shoved off. You can't get much more shoved off than dead, pally. And have we been introduced?"

"You don't know Mr. Bland?" Quill said.

"Why the hell should we know this guy?" Benny shook his head while ingesting the potatoes. He mumbled through the food. "Who is he again?"

"Neil Strickland's attorney," Quill said. "Everett Bland." She frowned. "You must have met him before."

"We've seen Mr. Bland on *Geraldo*," Ed said eagerly. "Attorney to the stars."

"And to JoyMax," Bland said equably. "I'd better see this show."

Quill smiled. "Coffee and dessert are in the conference room, gentlemen."

Mort hesitated. "I have to go up to my room for a sec."

"And there are other refreshments for those of you who don't care for coffee," Quill said.

"You got gin?"

"We have gin."

Mort led the way to the conference room and the men settled themselves around the table. All of them except Benny ignored the fruit sorbet set out on the sideboard. Everyone had coffee. Quill went to the head of the table and pulled down the white screen. "I guess I should turn this meeting over to the scriptwriting team. Would one of you care to chair the meeting?"

Eddie and Benny rose simultaneously. "Siddown, Ben. I got it." Eddie slouched to the TV. "Ladies and gentlemen, I give you the pilot for the all-new *Sneezer Show!*" He grinned happily. "This'll be good. You outsiders can give us feedback on this. Audience feedback always helps the studio." He killed the lights and turned on the VCR.

The screen flickered into life. The music came up. The intro was the overture from *Finlandia.* Quill guessed it was *Finlandia*; it was hard to tell since somebody had set it to hip-hop time.

MUSIC UP: (theme from *Finlandia,* rewritten for rappers.)

Scene 1, ext: Snow with blue sky above. SNEEZER, in a horned helmet and carrying a spear, is bobbing along the snow. His buddy the reindeer RALPH is trying to keep up. Periodically, they tumble over and over, falling into snowbanks, each other, etc.

VO: *(chorus of goofy voices)*

Way up north in the ice and snow . . .

Where only morons ever go!

SNEEZER and RALPH stop their dancing progress and inhale.

SNEEZER (bringing his head back! He's ready to sneeze, but not quite!!!): Ah-ah-ah . . .

CHORUS *(they're rappin'!)*

It's a duck!

It's a duck!

(He hasn't sneezed yet!! RALPH and SNEEZER romp on!)

CHORUS: *(they're rappin'!)*

He ain't too quick

But he ain't too slow!

SNEEZER: (he brings his head back to sneeze once again! This is going to be a good one!!)

AH-AH-AH-AH . . .

CHORUS:

He's a outta-luck duck

With the brains of a—

SFX: CHOO!

Scene 2: (CU) SNEEZER's finally sneezed! Snot
covers the screen, and music UP to cover the four-
letter word the censors won't let us use anyway!)

CHORUS: *SNEEZER!!!*

Eddie brought the lights up. Quill realized her mouth
was open and shut it. She didn't have the strength of
character to look at Horvath, but Marge, who had ti-
tanium nerves, could and did.

Horvath wheezed. He marched to the television and
removed the tape from the VCR. He opened the door
to the conference room and walked out. Quill got up
and followed him. She went into the hall and caught a
glimpse of him turning the corner to the bar. She followed slowly.

The bar was empty, except for Nate putting back the
polished and shining wineglasses. He placed each one
in a neat row on the shelf above the mahogany bartop.
It looked like a calm peaceful sort of job. The kind
that didn't involve soothing agitated investors. She
waved to Nate. Horvath was nowhere in sight.

"And so this is part of America," Horvath said into
her ear.

Quill whirled, tripped, and tumbled sideways. The
little Finn grabbed her elbow just in time. "Hi, Horvath!" she said rather breathlessly. "I suppose you're a
little upset."

"No." He shook his head decidedly. "I am not upset.
I am angry. Insults. Insults are part of America."

Quill took him by the arm. "Would you like a nice
drink? Let's sit down."

"You have seen this travesty of Finland before!" he demanded.

"No, I haven't. But Hagar—" She clapped her hand over her mouth. "Sorry. Sorry. I mean Horvath."

"*So!*" he roared. "Yet more mock is made of my country!" Horvath made a sound like "p-too!" "This is disgusting!"

"It's terrible," Quill agreed. "Horvath, I'm so sorry."

"You must throw these people from the Inn. My government will not allow such stuff."

"I don't blame you one bit for being angry."

"So you will throw them out?"

"I don't know if I can," she said honestly. "The police are still investigating this, um, accident to Mr. Strickland, and they may not . . ." She sighed hopelessly. "I'm so sorry!"

"Sorry is not enough. You are to throw them out. Immediately." He got up in a dignified way. "If you do not? Then I must say I have very many doubts about this deal."

"You know, I don't believe that Strickland would have let them air this show anyway," Quill said. "This is just a pilot, Horvath. Didn't they say that?"

"Yes. I have heard from other sources that the producer did not like this. But this producer is dead. And another Finn-hating producer may find this very funny. I do not. I shall call my embassy."

"You know," Quill said slowly, "I think that's what they mean for you to do."

"They would *like* an international incident over this? They will have an international incident over this. We Finns do not have the bomb, but we can get one. We are quite good friends with the Russians. Sometimes."

"Now hold on a minute, Horvath." Quill tugged him gently back into his chair. "I think we should have a vodka and talk about this."

"Vodka will not help."

"Stolyi?"

He grinned, albeit reluctantly. "You think I am—there is an American expression—"

"Overreacting?" She lifted her finger at Nate, who nodded comprehension. "No, I don't think you're overreacting."

Nate set a chilled bottle of Stolyi in front of them, with two shot glasses. Horvath poured. *"Prosit!"* He knocked it back. Quill knocked hers back and gasped. Horvath poured again. "To friendship!"

The third shot was to the business partnership between Finns and America. The fourth was in honor of the Finnish Revolution. Quill closed her eyes and sent a fierce mental message to Nate the bartender. She opened them. Nate kept on polishing wineglasses. Clearly he was concentrating too hard to receive them. "Nate!" she yelled as Horvath prepared a fifth shot of vodka.

Nate jumped. A wineglass crashed to the floor. "Ah, Quill?"

"Will you check on my . . . my . . ." Woozily she checked her watch. The hands danced. Had she found her Mickey Mouse watch after all these years? Tears came to her eyes. "Mickey!" she said.

"You okay, Quill?"

She blinked. Nate seemed to waver in and out of frame. She hoped that wasn't a horned helmet on his head; he moved and she realized he'd been in front of the moose head on the north wall.

"You wanted me to check on something?"

She thought hard. "My four o'clock appointment!" she said triumphantly. "Will you see if my four o'clock appointment is here? Wait . . . wait . . . I'll do it myself. In my office."

"Sherri Kerri's in your office, Quill." Dina said. The receptionist was here! Good old Dina! Quill started to laugh. "You two! You two look swimmy!"

". . . drunk!" Dina said.

". . . Stolyi." Nate's voice.

"Appointment," Quill said desperately. "My office." Somebody helped her up. "Too fast," Quill said clearly. "See you later, Hagar. After my a-point-ment."

". . . bed." That was Nate's slightly weary "bartender who'd seen it all" voice.

"She'll be madder if she doesn't keep her appointment," Dina said. "Quill, you're not that drunk, are you?"

"Absolutely not."

Dina helped her through the hallway, then an open door, and Quill recognized the peony-printed cushions of her couch. She sat down with a sigh and put her head between her knees. "Oh, my goodness."

"Is she okay? I stopped by to see if she's okay."

Quill twitched. That was Sherri Kerri. Had Dina made a mistake and taken her back to the gym? She didn't want to go back to the gym. She wailed, "I fell off the treadmill. And I'm not going back to the gym!" There were vague movements over her head. Someone was shaking hands with someone else.

"I'm Dina Muir. You must be Sherri. It is, like, so cool that you've opened a gym. And yeah, I think she's okay. Nate said she was drinking vodka with Horvath Kierkegaard, which is a mistake, because the guy has the constitution of a goat. I'm, like, not slamming the guy, or anything."

"Fourth rule," Quill moaned. "Don't call the guests names . . . excuse me, guys." She leaped from the couch and just made it to the small bathroom off her office.

She was very sick for what seemed like a very long time. She washed her face, brushed her teeth, and looked at herself in the mirror. The bruise over her left eye was from the treadmill. The pasty-white complexion . . . she thought of the green gunk and swallowed hard. A knock at the door roused her from mournful contemplation.

"Hey."

"Hey, Dina. Come in. No, wait, I'm coming out."

"You sure?"

"I'm sure." She pulled the door open. Sherri and Dina looked back at her. "I'm not drunk," Quill said clearly. "Just a little fuzzy. And I have to sit down."

The two of them leaped back. Quill wobbled to the couch and sank thankfully into it.

"You look awful," Dina said helpfully. "Can I get you anything?"

"She's got just the thing," Sherri said briskly. "I sold it to her yesterday." She raised her voice, *"Do you remember where you put your supplements?"*

Quill clapped her hands over her ear. "All I need is some tea. Really."

"I'll get it." Dina bit her lip. "You want some lemon?"

"Yes. And if you laugh at me, you're fired."

"Not in a million years."

Quill, eyes closed, heard Dina leave, and the quiet sounds of someone still in her office. "Sherri?"

"Right here! You going to be sick again?"

"No. But I have words of wisdom to offer. Never drink with a Finn." She opened her eyes. Sherri stared at her with disapproval. "I don't do this, you know. Get drunk at four in the afternoon."

Sherri made an "of course not" noise.

"It was because . . . Oh, never mind." She pushed herself upright with a groan.

"It's a good thing to vomit," Sherri said seriously. "Gets all the toxins out of your system."

"I feel better." She looked at the cciling. It was pierced tin and she'd always liked it. "Actually I don't feel better. I just don't feel drunk." She rolled her head slightly. "I meant to tell you I was sorry about barging in on you last night."

"No problem."

"Is he nice?" Quill said a little wistfully. "Sorry, I don't mean to pry. I'm a little envious of people who have their love lives straightened out."

"Sometimes you don't choose it," Sherri said distantly. "It just chooses you."

"That helps with the decision," Quill said wryly. "Is there anything I can do for you?"

"I dropped by to see if you were okay after falling off the treadmill. And I didn't have any more clients scheduled, so I thought I'd take a look at the Inn. I haven't been here yet, and everyone talks about it. It's great. Kind of old, but great."

"I'm glad you did." Quill tried to inject some warmth into her voice, which was hard, since Sherri was so bouncingly *there*. Health, high energy, and tan combined to give her a golden nimbus. She strode around the small space like a V-8 engine strapped to a lawn mower. She poked at the little ivory unicorn on Quill's desk, picked up a cloisonné bowl Quill had owned for years, and examined her photographs. "This your folks?"

"Yes. It was taken a year before they died."

"Your father's really handsome. Looks like one of those old-time Shakespearean actors. Olivier, maybe. Or Barrymore."

"My sister takes after him. I take after my mother."

Sherri dropped the photo with a clunk and craned her neck at the walls. She cracked her knuckles; her arms rippled with healthy muscle. Quill wondered if she'd have such a hangover if she were buff. Probably not. "What about your pictures?" Sherri asked. "I don't see any in here. You paint, don't you?"

Quill replied as she always did when people asked her this question. "A little."

"My father says you're pretty good. I thought maybe I'd see if you wanted to have me display some of your smaller ones at the gym. Kind of a quid pro quo for keeping the flyers at the desk."

Quill felt another stab of empathy for Horvath. "Does your father paint?"

"You mean why would he know who you are when I don't? Dad's one of those up-to-the-minute guys.

He's in business, too. Although," she said candidly, "he's rich and I'm not. Is your dad rich?"

"My parents died when I was sixteen. How did we get off on this?" Quill said pleasantly.

Sherri chuckled. "I don't know. I was worried that you really smacked yourself on the treadmill, and that I'd been too pushy about having you join the gym, and I don't know you well enough to apologize, so I guess I was babbling."

Dina tapped on the door and pushed it open with her knee. She carried a loaded tea tray. Quill was extremely thirsty. Dina set the tray down and poured three cups. She gave the first to Quill, served Sherri and herself, and perched on the edge of the desk.

Sherri sat on the opposite end of the couch and said, "There's one more reason I dropped by. How much do you want for the Inn?"

CHAPTER 8

"Is there some sort of weird genetic experiment going on we don't know about?" Quill asked John the next morning at breakfast. "The kind that makes people totally nuts?"

John laughed. He had a nice laugh, low and easy.

They sat at the manager's table in the dining room. Early-morning sun poured in through the floor-to-ceiling windows. Quill was exhausted; the echo of the vodka was still in her system.

She yawned. "Sorry. Anyway, I told Sherri Kerri thank you very much, but we were pretty sure that the deal with Horvath is going to go through." She folded and refolded the linen napkin. "It is going to go through, isn't it? I mean, even if Strickland's lawyer sues us?"

Everett Bland sat near them, eating a plate of salmon

scrambled eggs. John turned a little so he could see him. "I don't know. But I really doubt Sherri Kerri has the wherewithal to make a better offer."

"Oh, she wasn't going to offer cash, John. Just shares in her business. She said she's already picked up a partner. Mort Carmody, if you can believe it. He came by the gym, liked what he saw, and asked to sign on. She says she's planning on a huge expansion. I don't know where she's going to get enough customers in Hemlock Falls, but some business people just seem to know how to make money. The scriptwriters certainly seemed to have faith in her."

"Is the gym on Main Street the only one she owns?"

"You're not serious!"

"Being good at business is a talent, Quill. If we can raise enough money on her shares, we ought to look at all options."

"I'd sooner have *Bland* as a partner," Quill spluttered.

Bland had copped the best table, number seven, which overlooked the Gorge and the waterfall. He was dressed in a three-piece linen suit, a dark blue shirt, and a club tie. Horvath walked into the dining room and joined him.

"You don't like her?"

"She's fine. She's just so—I don't know. Wound up. All those supplements and the workouts. I know what it is," she said darkly. She sipped her tomato juice. "She makes me feel guilty. The super-fit always make me feel guilty. And she's . . ."

"What?"

Got her love life straightened out, Quill thought. I'm

such a *jerk*! "Nothing. She's one of those super-successful people who knows what she wants and is cheerful about deserving it. One of those people for whom life is easy. I'm just jealous."

"I'll keep that in mind. Any word from the sheriff's department on the cause of Strickland's death?"

"I thought I'd give Davey Kiddermeister a call this morning. It hasn't occurred to him yet that he shouldn't be giving me information. John, did you know that Bland knows Horvath? From way back, he said."

John took a sip of juice. "How far back?"

"I don't know. Horvath seems to make lifelong friends after six minutes, so it could be as recently as last week. But he knows Bland as a real-estate lawyer. What's going on here? I thought Bland was here to represent Strickland's estate."

"Let me make a few phone calls this morning. I'll try and find out more about him. But if he is interested in buying the Inn, it doesn't preclude any case he might have on Strickland's behalf." He paused. "Or maybe it does. Do you know much about him?"

"I don't even know how old he is," Quill said frankly. "Not that that matters a hill of beans. I've stopped trying to peg how old people from L.A. are." She continued darkly. "Some plastic surgeons have a lot to answer for. People from L.A. all want to look the best age for making money. Look at Mr. Bland. You'd say he was a healthy fifty. But who knows?"

"He's sixty-five," Meg said as she bounced in from the kitchen. She set a bowl of blueberries and cream in front of John, then sat down opposite Quill. She was dressed in light chinos and a thin silk blouse. "Doreen saw him on *Sally Jesse*."

Quill rubbed her eyes. "Celebrity lawyers. Dead producer. If this gets any worse, we'll have about three seconds until the media arrive. This kind of mess is just too good for them to pass up. And I look like a toad."

"You look beautiful," John said. "I'll run into Syracuse this morning, Quill. I'll check in with a couple of friends at the newspaper office. They may have a file on Strickland and Everett Bland."

"What if Bland does want to buy into the Inn? Doesn't that help our position with the Finns? I mean, if there's another possible investor, that can only help us, can't it?"

John turned his head slightly and gave Bland a measuring look. Horvath had joined him. The two men talked earnestly. "Depends a great deal on what Bland is really after. And we won't know that for a while."

Quill ran her hands despairingly through her hair. "I don't know if I can deal with all of this right now. Even if Strickland died from a fall, Bland is going to sue us and my dog. And that translates into very bad publicity, which is going to affect the Finns, who are already mightily annoyed over the *Sneezer* debacle. Is there any way we can keep the news anchors and the radio types and the journalists from descending on us like a cloud of locusts? Especially when I look like a locust."

Meg said kindly, "You need a haircut. And a little makeup wouldn't hurt."

"It melts in the heat," Quill said mournfully. She put

her forefingers at her temples and pulled up. "And my face is falling off."

"Your face doesn't fall off at thirty-six," Meg said. "Now, when you hit forty, major slump."

John smiled. "I see you two have things straightened out."

"Just in time, too," Doreen said.

Quill jumped in her chair. "I wish you wouldn't sneak *up* on me, Doreen!"

"Then I wouldn't hear much, would I?" The housekeeper sniffed disapprovingly and took the last chair at the table. Quill poured her a cup of coffee, and she waved it away. "Got things to do this morning. Chamber meetin' at ten, and you got a train to catch, Meg."

Meg looked at her watch, muttered, and got up to leave. "We've got to find out about Strickland and get this whole affair cleared up. Everything's stalled until then—I've already talked to Andrew about putting off the ceremony another week. I'll call home tonight. With any luck, I'll have those background checks on Strickland for you."

"I'll have the timetable ready."

Doreen watched Meg leave with a disapproving stare then turned her beady eye on Quill. "What background check? What timetable? For where them three scriptwriters were at when Strickland was killed? You two back in the detective business?"

"We can't let them pin this murder on Max, Doreen," Quill said a little defensively. "And last night Meg and I decided to handle Strickland's death in a professional way. I'm going to find out from the Three Stooges when and where they were at the time the corpse ended up at the foot of the Gorge."

"Sheriff can do any background checks you want."

Quill sipped her coffee, which was cold. "Meg's got a contact at the restaurant."

Doreen nodded. "A-huh. So who's this pal of Meg's?"

Quill grinned. "Well, it's the busboy. But he's a terrific computer hacker, and Meg says he can get into the L.A. police files like that." She snapped her fingers. "If Strickland got so much as a jaywalking ticket in the past ten years, Meg says this kid will find out. And Myles isn't on this investigation, Doreen. He left last night for a conference in Seattle. Captain Harris is going to be taking this case over."

Doreen snorted. "*That* bozo. I remember him from the cattle case."

A smile lit John's face. Suddenly he was young. "Are we keeping case files now, Doreen?"

Doreen sat up in the chair. Her hair all but bristled with excitement. "You know," she said in a low, confidential tone, "that ain't such a bad idea. Writin' up them files. That Rex Stout musta made a mint. "And they put that Nero Wolfe on TV. That's where the money is. TV scripts!"

"No!" John and Quill said simultaneously.

Quill, remembering Doreen's forays into Amway, fundamentalist religion, and various other enthusiasms, shuddered at the thought of Doreen Muxworthy-Stoker, mystery writer. "Why not gardening? Or cross-stitch?"

"Huh." Doreen, her multitude of housekeeping chores forgotten, smacked her lips in excitement. "You know, the thing is, your basic mystery detective has to *do* something. To keep it interesting, like."

"Do something?" Quill shook her head, as if to clear cobwebs. "Do what? Detectives are usually part of the police. Or the FBI."

"Not the interesting ones. The interesting ones eat, maybe. Like that there Nero Wolfe. Or raise dogs or cats. Or run a catering service. Now, I wonder . . ."

"While you're wondering, why don't you supervise the setup for the Chamber of Commerce brunch," Quill suggested. "They'll be here in two hours, and please let Bjarne know they'll be three extra. In the meantime I'm going to find the scriptwriters. I've got some questions for them."

"You watch yourself," Doreen said. "It's gotta be one a them. Nobody from Hemlock Falls had any reason to whack Strickland."

Quill found the three easily enough. They were sitting outside on the flagstone terrace near the Tavern Lounge. They were drinking orange juice. Someone, probably Bjarne, had filled the buffet table against the wall with fruit, pastries, and juice. Quill caught the distinctive scent of gin.

"It's the beautiful redhead," Mort Carmody said. He shoved an empty wrought-iron chair with his toe. "Have a seat."

Quill sat down. Mort, she decided, was the one with the gin. He had a cigarette and a large cup of coffee in addition to his juice. Ed bit his nails and ignored his glass. Benny scraped at the remains of Meg's blintzes.

"I bet you wonder why I'm drinking gin at eight-thirty in the morning." Mort leaned over the glass-topped table. His eyes were brown, with yellow veins streaking the whites. "I'll just bet you are."

"Why are you?" Quill asked pleasantly. Guilty conscience? she wanted to add. Sleepless nights? Do you keep hearing the shrieks of your victim as he tumbled over the edge of Hemlock Gorge?

"I keep hearing the shrieks," Mort said. Tears filled his eyes.

"Ahem," Quill said. She had frequently thought it would be a good idea to carry a concealed tape recorder. One just never knew. "Would you like to talk about it?" she asked kindly.

"I *am* going to be talking about it!" Mort said. His face flushed. "And talking and talking and talking about it. I won't get a chance to shut up about it."

"Shut up now, why don't you?" Ed Schwartz had been wearing his sunglasses on the top of his head. He shoved them down over his eyes and said in a bored way, "Have another gin. Save the loquacity for the meeting."

"You know, Mort." Quill resisted the temptation to put a sympathetic hand on his. He looked sweaty. "We can arrange for a lawyer. There's quite a few in Syracuse."

"Lawyers are the worst," Benny said. "Every goddamn one of 'em thinks he can write a screenplay. Jesus Christ. As if we don't have enough trouble with that damn Finn and that big-assed broad with the hat."

Quill counted to ten. She decided that (a) she disliked Benny, Mort, and Ed almost as much as she had disliked their dead producer, and (b) Mort was not confessing to the murder of Neil Strickland, but to something else. "What's going on? Guys." She added the noun in a friendlier tone. Rule Two of the innkeeper's code was don't annoy the guests unless absolutely necessary. (Rule One was don't belt the guests; it had been Rule Five up to the time they'd hired Doreen.)

"Well, there was quite a crowd here after they found Neil's body," Mort said. He sucked deeply on his cigarette. "Whole village must have been here."

"Murders are interesting," Quill said feebly. "And there's not a lot going on at the moment in town."

"Big woman with a hat? Garden-club type? She's the mayor, I think."

"Married to the mayor," Quill said. "Adela Henry. What about her?"

"Asked Mort here to make a presentation to the Chamber of Commerce meeting this morning. And before we knew it, we'd agreed to a little writers' workshop sort of thing. This afternoon. In your conference room."

"Turns out Mrs. Mayor has an idea for a TV show," Ed said mournfully.

"Everybody has an idea for a TV show," Benny added. "If not an actual treatment." He looked a little nervously at Quill. "You don't, do you?"

Quill shook her head. So that's what was behind Doreen's latest enthusiasm.

"Thing is, Mrs. Mayor said she'd pay us the going rate." Ed's watery blue eyes were hopeful. "Might be a business in it, Benny. And God knows we all could use the money if *Sneezer*'s canceled—"

"Shut up, you moron!" Mort hissed.

"If the cartoon show is canceled?" Quill asked innocently. "Is that likely to happen?"

"Absolutely not!" Benny said firmly. "We're in the top fifty of kids' shows."

"If there were forty-nine others out there, you'd be right," Mort snarled. He threw his cigarette on the flagstones and lit another. "What the hell, it was all Neil's fault. He had the taste of a goat. Now that Neil's gone, you watch. We'll get *Sneezer* back in the top ten."

Benny glared at him. "Have another gin, jerk. And after that, go e-mail that clot Harris with your motive."

"Surely you guys aren't under suspicion!" Quill widened her eyes. "Did you say something about Captain Harris? Does he think you wanted to kill Mr. Strickland?"

"Anybody who knew Neil wanted to kill him," Ed said succinctly. "And yeah, some state trooper put the screws to us yesterday morning when we went to give depositions. Seems to think we're the most likely suspects."

Quill shook her head sympathetically. "You can account for your whereabouts during the relevant times, can't you?"

Benny brushed cheese-blintz filling from his chinos and ignored her question. "We saw how that dog went for him the first time—at your instigation, I might add. We practically saw that damn dog attack him the second time. But that didn't seem to get through Captain Harris's thick skull."

"You saw Max?" Quill crossed one leg over the other. She grabbed her bare ankle and pinched it so she wouldn't lose her temper. "When was that?"

"Everyone saw Max," Ed Schwartz said glumly. "That skinny broad with the frizzy gray hair? Looks like a rooster? Gave the dog a bath, I guess, and he tore through the bar like a banshee, with the skin—"

"Her name is Mrs. Stoker," Quill snapped. "And she's a friend of mine."

"Friend of yours? Sorry. Anyway, Mrs. Stoker was chasing him and she chased him right out the back doors and onto the lawn. He skedaddled over the lip of the Gorge and disappeared."

"You can't see the lip of the Gorge from the Tavern Bar," Quill said.

Eddie wriggled his shoulders. "Mort and I were kinda cheering for the dog, if you know what I mean. We got up and opened the French doors for him. That lady had a broom!"

"What time was this?"

Mort and Ed exchanged bewildered looks. "Damned if I know." Mort drew heavily on his third cigarette, then tossed it onto the flagstone floor. "Some while after Neil left."

"Nate'd know, probably," Benny said. "Good barkeep, that Nate."

Quill cocked her head. "You know—it's Benny, isn't it? You look familiar."

He smiled self-deprecatingly. "You might have seen me on one of the afternoon talk shows. I do a bit of interview work now and then."

"I don't watch afternoon talk shows," Quill said. "No, I've seen you in Hemlock Falls, I'm almost sure of it."

"Well, yeah. I stayed here a couple of years ago.

You might not remember, you had a wedding here—it was the week that Senator Alphonse Santini was killed."

"Yes," Quill said hastily. "That was quite a week. I was tied up. I'm pretty bad on names, but I don't forget faces." She drew a breath to ask the next question: had Benny been a wedding guest? Because if he had, he was going to shoot to the top of her suspect list. Practically everyone associated with that dismal wedding had been connected to organized crime. Now, there was a lead. "So is that why the four of you decided to come here? At your suggestion?"

"Seemed like a good, quiet place to work," Benny said. "But no, the idea came from Neil's lawyer."

"Everett Bland?"

"Everett Bland? You're kidding, right? Neil's potatoes were way too small for someone like Bland. Nah, his lawyer is with some big firm on the Strip. Dewey, Cheetam and Howe." Mort's laugh turned into a phlegmy cough.

So they hadn't met Bland. And this was odd. Maybe even a clue. Quill took another deep breath. "Do you know the law firm's real name?"

"Hel-lo-oo!" a voice caroled invitingly. Adela Henry stumped around the corner of the building and onto the terrace. Doreen and Marge Schmidt trudged behind her. "There you all are!" Adela beamed. She was wearing a gauzy white hat with a wide brim and a bright teal pantsuit. Doreen had exchanged her print dress for jeans, a black turtleneck, and a tweed jacket. Quill instantly recognized this as Doreen's writer's uniform. Both Doreen and Adela were carrying manila envelopes. Only Marge looked reassuringly normal, in khaki pants and a baggy T-shirt. And she wasn't carrying anything suspiciously manuscriptlike.

"This writing workshop is so exciting," Adela said. "We're all gathered and waiting, gentlemen."

Mort emptied his gin and orange with a single swallow. Ed looked at his feet. Benny muttered, "Jesus!" Then: "You have the registration fees collected?"

"Right here." Adela was nothing if not efficient. She handed over a thick envelope. "Some of the students didn't have enough cash on them, so I took checks. I know you said no checks, but it's Saturday, and most people have to go to Syracuse to get that amount because the bank's closed and the ATM only lets you take out two hundred dollars at a time."

Benny ignored her. He fanned through the contents of the envelope. Then he got up and shook hands with each woman in turn. "Benny Gilpin," he said. "Delighted to meet you all."

"It can't be ten o'clock already," Quill said, knowing very well it was nine-fifteen. "And I thought that the workshop was set for this afternoon? Doreen, why don't you take Marge and Adela into the dining room for some coffee until it's time for the Chamber meeting? Meg baked this morning." Adela clutched her manila envelope. "Crullers," Quill added.

Adela swallowed. Doreen made shooing motions. "You go on, Adela. I got a lot to talk to Benny about."

"I'm sure you do," Adela said stiffly, "but I hardly think that Mr. Gilpin and his confreres are going to be interested in *your* idea for a TV series." She raised her eyebrows. "Her detective is a housekeeper for a twenty-seven-room inn in upstate New York. Quite uncreative, don't you think?" She smiled at Benny, who took two involuntary steps backward into the patio table. "Now, my little idea should have a much broader appeal than Doreen's."

Mort sidled behind Ed; they both stepped nervously off the terrace and onto the lawn. Benny scratched his ear casually and positioned himself behind Mort. The three men looked like cooped chickens with a fox on the loose.

Quill gave in to her better nature and intervened. "It might be better to wait until the official start of the workshop, Adela. I'm going to have to insist that we follow, um . . . protocol." Adela was big on protocol.

"She don't want to wait," Doreen scoffed. "She wants to get her horn in ahead of everyone. She always does. You're pushy, Adela. You always have been."

"Everyone else?" Mort asked in a hollow way. "How many others are there?"

"Not mor'n seven or eight," Doreen said. "I know Harvey Bozzel's draggin' around an idea he's had for more years than he's been an adman. And the Reverend Shuttleworth's got a plan for a TV show about a kids' choir, and Esther's detective runs a dress shop. And Freddie Bellini came up with somethin' like *Calling Hours*."

"Freddie's our funeral director," Quill explained to the scriptwriters. "I expect his detective's a mortician."

"Ay-uh," Doreen said. "Get a lot of plot ideas outta that. What with enough bodies and all."

"Are all the script ideas for mystery shows?" Quill asked.

"Heck no," Doreen said. "Harvey's got some damnfool notion of a show called *Adman!* Main guy in it is an advertising guy who's actually an alien." She scowled ferociously. "Now, there's those what think something like that's gonna fly, but I think it's stupid. You gonna have an alien as a main character, you want the alien to be somethin' more interesting than an adman. An FBI agent, maybe, where they get into more interesting situations than selling Campbell's soup."

"Been done," Marge grunted. "Got a show already where the alien's an FBI man."

"That FBI man is not an alien," Doreen said in the patient tones one uses to tell a three-year-old not to eat dirt. "That FBI man *is* an FBI man. He chases aliens."

"I think if you have a show with an alien," Adela said, "that the character of the alien should be a physician. A show with that would have legs."

"Legs?" Doreen was clearly bewildered.

"Legs," Adela repeated, with an infuriatingly wise air. "That show *ER* would boost its rating enormously if they had an alien on staff."

"*Emergency Room Alien*?" Mort muttered. "Have to be. No. Maybe *Emergency Alien*." His mournful donkey expression brightened. "Long as it's not *Emergency Alien Room*, you might have something there, Mrs. er—um—"

"Dell Henry," Adela said briskly. "I was figuring how my name should look in the credits and I think Dell Henry has punch."

"You want a punch, Adela," Doreen said in a threatening way. "I'd be glad to oblige you."

"Stop," Quill said. "Right now."

There was a startled silence.

"We are all going to the Chamber of Commerce meeting," Quill said firmly. "And we're going to sit through it as we always do, and afterward you can sit down and squabble to your hearts' content over these ideas, but *not now*!"

"For goodness' sake." Adela frowned thoughtfully. "Of course, you can sit down and talk to these gentlemen anytime you want to, Sarah Quilliam, anytime of the day or night," she added with unmistakable malice. "I surely don't think you would begrudge us a little time to talk to these gentlemen off-line."

"Any time of the day or night, baby!" Mort leered hopefully at her.

Quill wheeled around, slammed through the French doors to the Tavern Bar, and from there down the hall past their small conference room into the front foyer. Dina sat behind the reception desk, reading. She looked up as Quill stomped in. "Anything wrong?"

Quill tugged furiously at her hair. It was supposed to be hot today, and she'd pinned it up. The heavy coils fell over her shoulders, scattering pins and clips. She swept it back up and jammed a couple of pins back into it.

Dina narrowed her eyes. "It's lopsided," she said briskly.

"It's always lopsided. I'm going to cut it off."

"Sit down and I'll fix it for you. I want to talk to you anyhow, and there's always so many people around it's impossible."

Quill sighed and went past the receptionist desk into her office. Dina followed her and carefully closed the door. Quill pulled a brush out of the top drawer of her desk and sat down. Dina unpinned her hair and brushed it out with brisk, competent strokes. "Shall I do French braids? I've practiced a lot on my sisters."

"Sure," Quill said. "Whatever you want. Just don't tell me you're going to quit."

"Quit? I don't want to quit. Being around here is better than TV. Although I could use a raise, now that you mention it."

"I don't recall mentioning it," Quill said. "I'll do better than a raise. You can be president of the Inn, how's that?"

"President, huh."

"Sure. You get to deal with the guests, my loony sister, Doreen, the whole Chamber of Commerce—"

"Sheriff McHale?" Dina asked.

Quill tilted her head back and glared.

Dina grinned, unperturbed. "Not the sheriff. John Raintree, then?" She started to braid Quill's hair back and forth. Quill felt like a loom.

"Why doesn't anybody quake in their boots when I'm around? I'm the boss. I can fire people like that." She snapped her fingers. "I'm a woman of substance. A woman of property. When Marge Schmidt stomps into a room, everyone sits up straight and salutes. And they'd salute even if she had fifty cents in her bank account rather than fifty million or whatever it is. Adela Henry gets away with saying whatever she wants to whomever she wants. Doreen whacks people with her broom. But nobody listens to me!"

"Hmm. There's a little gray in here. You might want to think about a nice red-gold rinse next time you go to get your hair done."

"Dina!"

"Hang on, Quill. I'm almost finished." She pushed the last hairpin in place and stood back, smiling. "Take a look."

Quill took a small hand mirror from the desk drawer. She couldn't see the back, but the French braids made a nice line off her temples. "Thank you. It's lovely. You're fired."

"Right. Quill, have you seen *The Sneezer show!*?"

"Yes."

"Well, you'd better watch this one. You know how Sneezer used to be this little black duck?"

"I've seen it. Some of it. Does it get better after he sneezes all over the screen?" she said hopefully.

"As if! He's this duck. Like Daffy Duck, only ugly. He used to be a streetwise duck with a smart mouth. Now he's a streetwise duck with a smart mouth who's a Finn."

"Yep."

"A Finn!" Dina continued in high dudgeon. "A rude, stupid, obnoxious, politically incorrect Finn. It's horrible. In the show I saw with Doreen—well, all I can say is that it's worse than the show they got sued over."

This Quill didn't know. She sat up. "The *Sneezer* people have been sued before? By whom?"

"Everyone. The ACLU, the skinheads, the American Dental Association . . . and they lost, big time. It's an awful show. It's worse than *Beavis and Butt-head*."

Quill rubbed her nose thoughtfully. "Has Horvath seen all of it?"

"Not yet. But he's signed up for that scriptwriting seminar, and the scriptwriters asked for a VCR in the conference room where the seminar is supposed to be held this afternoon, and it's because that Mort person is going to show their work first to demonstrate the right way to do a cartoon series, I guess, and—"

"Wow," Quill said. "Oh, wow. Horvath's going to blow his top if that whole tape is run in front of God and everybody. Yikes! Tell you what, Dina. When you go into the conference room to check the coffee setup, swipe that tape."

"And?"

"I don't know. We'll hold it hostage or something. Good grief."

"Stealing? You want me to steal?"

"I want you to relocate the tape. Somewhere else. Like maybe Buffalo. Otherwise it's all the excuse Horvath needs to back out."

"We need that money, don't we? From the Finns."

"You bet we do." Quill jumped to her feet. "Why in the world is Horvath going to the workshop anyway?"

"He's got a script idea, he says, about a Finn who's a detect—"

"Aaagh!" Quill clutched her hair. Dina shrieked. Quill's braids fell down. Dina shoved her back into the chair and began to pin them up. "Another detective?" Quill asked plaintively

"People love detectives," Dina said cheerfully. "There. Now if you can keep from shrieking and clutching your hair, you'll be fine."

"Is that why people don't stand up and salute when I walk into a room? Because I shriek and clutch my hair?"

Dina shook her head. "It's because you let people get away with murder, Quill. You don't have a temper. You have anxiety attacks. You get bemused. You get insecure. But you don't get mad, not Meg's kind of mad, and you don't threaten unmentionable reprisals, like that horrible Carol Ann, and you don't get superior like Marge."

"Marge *is* superior," Quill muttered. "She has more money than God and she made it all herself."

"The worst thing is your sense of humor. Nobody's afraid of someone with a sense of humor. Like you saying 'you're fired' to me a few seconds ago. As if!"

"Well, you are fired," Quill said crossly. The little clock on her desktop chimed the hour and she groaned. "But not till after this damn Chamber meeting. Look. After about twenty minutes you come in with an urgent message for me."

"If you have an urgent message, you should take care of it now."

"A pretend urgent message. I've got a ton of stuff to do today and no time for the meeting."

"But who's going to take notes? You're the secretary."

"You'll take notes," Quill said ruthlessly. "And that's an order. But the first thing is to get Max out of dog jail. I've got to talk to Howie about how to accomplish that. And then I have to find out who murdered that miserable Neil Strickland."

"Piece of cake," Dina said. "You've done it before and you can do it again. Just *don't touch your hair*!"

"I love your hair!" Miriam Doncaster shrieked as Quill walked into the conference room a few moments later. The librarian gave her an impulsive hug. Quill reined in the impulse to shriek back. Shrieking and hugging were Pavlovian responses among women greeting one another. Somewhere between her office and the meeting room, she'd decided that her life was a disorderly mess because no one respected her. She didn't know if gender had anything to do with it, but she was *not* going to be the sort of person who (a) people such as her sister didn't tell things to, and (b) left assorted lovers in ambiguous positions, and (c) got hollered at by mayors' wives. So she didn't shriek back at Miriam, but she did hug her. Temperately. And in a very dignified way.

The long mahogany conference table was crowded with Chamber members. Summertime usually meant a decline in attendance. Quill noticed that most of the members who normally had unbreakable appointments (at the golf course) or heavy-duty meetings (in their gardens) that kept them from July and August meetings were there. Most held a variety of briefcases, manila folders, oversized handbags stuffed with manuscripts, or (in the case of Freddie Bellini) gold-embossed leather scrapbooks. TV scripts, naturally. She thought of the gin-swilling Mort and doleful Eddie Schwartz and grinned.

"You seem pretty chipper for a person with another body on the premises," Esther West said tartly. She smoothed a curl stiff with hairspray over her left ear. "Unless you have some news you want to share with us. About a certain set of scriptwriters, maybe?"

"Nice to see you, too, Esther," Quill said.

"I've been thinking I ought to just check right into the Inn, Quill," Miriam said as Quill sat down next to her. "I mean, propinquity gives a person terrific advantage. And they do say it's who you know."

"Who says that about what?" Quill asked. "If you guys are talking about the possibility of selling your script ideas to those men from L.A., I have to say I think it's pretty remote."

"Well, you would say that, wouldn't you?" Esther said. "Don't want any competition." She tugged her white patent-leather belt into place, then smoothed her black-and-white-checked skirt over her knees. Esther ran the best (and only) dress shop in Hemlock Falls, but her taste in her own clothes never varied: full skirts, broad belts, and large plastic earrings. "I mean, there's very few spots available on prime-time TV."

"Cable," Freddie Bellini interjected from across the table. "Cable's the way to go now. I heard that HBO is buying." He smoothed the top of his leather portfolio.

"Heard from whom?" Quill asked. She had not, she told herself, been transported to an alternate reality. These were people she'd known for years.

"It was in this week's *TV Guide*," Esther said briskly, "Average price for a first sale is around fifty k. And don't pretend you don't know it, missy. I think Freddie's right. I think I should check into the Inn while the gentlemen from L.A. are here."

"We're not really licensed to open yet," Quill said.

"So you say," Esther snapped. "But all's fair in love and TV, isn't it, Quill?"

Quill closed her eyes and counted to ten. The mayor saved her from a tart rejoinder with a thwack of the gavel against the mahogany tabletop.

"This Chamber meetin' is now open," he declared. "Madame Secretary, would you read the minutes from the last meeting?"

Quill sat up. She blushed. So much for her decision to behave like a competent executive. "Um. I'll have to go get them, Elmer. They're in my office. I think. Or maybe they're still in my room, I was transcribing them a few—"

Elmer waved his hand. "No matter. No matter. We only got a few items on the table anyhow. First one is the report from the Ladies' Auxiliary, given by my lady-wife." He looked around the table. "Adela?"

"She's still out back, Elmer," Quill said. "Would you like me to go get her?" No, that wasn't at all in the executive manner. "That is, I'll send someone to fetch her." She straightened her shoulders and raised her chin.

"Sure," Elmer said agreeably.

There was a short silence. A respectful silence. Quill would have enjoyed the respect a lot more if she'd had someone to send to find Adela. "Um. I'll be back in just a second."

"Hold on now." Harland Peterson held up a large, beefy hand. Harland had the bluff, outdoor complexion of the farmer (which he was) and the confidence of a well-fixed man in charge of three employees and goodness knows how many acres of corn, wheat, and red beans. (He was that as well.) "Just where was Adela when you last saw her, Quill?"

"On the terrace with Mort Carmody, Benny Gilpin, and Eddie Schwartz. It's just a few steps from here, Harland. I'll be glad to get her."

"Hmm." Harland rubbed his chin. "No use disturbing her if she's got a little business goin'." He shifted in his chair. A fat roll of manuscript paper peeked from the back pocket of his dark green cotton trousers. "Why don't you go on to the next item of business, Mayor?"

"Right. Next item is the Chamber of Commerce tent for the Wine Festival in September. We still need a pack of volunteers . . . you goin', Harland?"

"Forgot something," the farmer said airily. He sidled his way between the table and the occupied chairs to the door.

"So did I," Esther said. She sprang up. She followed Harland out the door.

"Well! I must say that I wouldn't disgrace myself by running after those men no matter how much money and fame were at stake!" Miriam said. She drummed her fingers on the tabletop. "The seminar's scheduled for one o'clock, right after lunch, and I for one am not about to miss Meg's food!"

"She's not cooking today," Betty Hall said from her usual spot by the corner wall. She had been Marge's partner in the late (and much-lamented) Hemlock Home Diner and an excellent chef. Quill had no idea how Betty found out Meg's whereabouts, but she always knew. "That Bjarne's cooking. He is," Betty added grudgingly, "a decent man with fish. But that's about it."

"Quill's lunches are always wonderful," Miriam said stoutly. "Shall we strive for a little dignity here, Mayor? I'd like the meeting to go forward."

The mayor clapped his gavel against the tabletop once again. Harvey Bozzel slipped out so quickly Quill barely caught a glimpse of the rear side of his Dockers. As Elmer continued with his plea for volunteers for the festival tent, the room gradually emptied, until the only Chamber members present were the mayor, Miriam, and the Reverend Dookie Shuttleworth, who stared benignly at the mayor and whose thoughts (as usual) drifted gently in some cloud-cuckoo-land of his own invention.

"Quill and I will be happy to volunteer for the festival tent," Miriam said. "And Pastor D? What about you? Will you have time to help out?"

Dookie nodded, and kept on nodding.

Quill stopped herself from tugging her hair.

"I, for one, intend to sit through this whole meeting, as we all should," Miriam declared. "Some people may think that backing certain other people into corners and haranguing them with certain ideas for screenplays is going to work to their advantage. All I have to say is that gentility will out." She tapped Quill's shoulder in a highly irritating way. "Gentility will out."

The door to the conference room opened. Miriam smiled in satisfaction. "See? I don't even have to look around. Those poor men sent all those greedy, ill-mannered persons packing."

"Am I too late?" Sherri Kerri asked. "Is the Chamber meeting over?"

Quill turned and greeted her with a smile. "You made it! Mayor? Have you met Sherri Kerri?"

Elmer extended his hand and shook Sherri's heartily. "Always glad to meet a new member of the business community. Heard a lot about you. Glad to have you with us. The wife is goin' to sign up for your classes, if she hasn't already."

"The lady with the flowered hat?" Sherri said briskly. "I put her in the Sensuous Seniors class."

Elmer's scant eyebrows rose in alarm. He glanced nervously at the Reverend Shuttleworth. "The, ah—huh?"

"We have a class for full-figured ladies," Sherri said. "We start 'em off slowly, Mayor, and at the end of six weeks—*whoosh!* My exercise class restores vitality and energy of all kinds, for all women!"

"Quill?" Dina edged into the conference room. Quill was glad to see that her face was appropriately pale, as befitted the bearer of an urgent message. "I really, really think you ought to come out here."

Quill had rehearsed her response in her mind. Too bad there were only three Chamber members (and one of them new) to see it. She cleared her throat in an executive way and pointed her forefinger at Dina, in the same way she imagined Donald Trump fielded questions from Don King. "Wait for me," she said grandly.

"I can't. The police captain says right now."

Quill felt herself deflate. "Harris?" she asked, rather feebly for a senior executive.

"Although it won't make any difference to poor Mr. Carmody whether you're late or not." Dina continued, nodding sadly. "Yes, Quill. He's dead."

CHAPTER 9

Quill hated the word *rictus*. It sounded just like Carmody looked—contorted, strained—a death-grin word. She eyed the body in the lawn chair. Mort Carmody was as unlovely in death as he had been in life. He was intolerably pitiful. He slumped backward, mouth and eyes wide open to the hot August sky, arms dangling. His orange-juice glass lay shattered on the flagstones.

Quill scanned the crowd near the body and found Marge in front, hands shoved into her pockets, her face a mask. Quill caught her eye. Marge nodded and ambled over.

"Marge, where are Adela and Doreen?"

"That trooper Harris is interrogating them," Marge said. "Doreen gave Howie a call beforehand, and he's headed over, so she's goin' to be okay, Quill. Don't get your knickers in a twist."

"What happened?"

"Poison," Marge said in her ear. "In the gin, I believe."

"You noticed he was drinking? So did I."

Marge snorted. "Can't be in the restaurant business and not know a drunk when I see one, Quill." She stood staring at the body, feet planted squarely on the ground, her head thrust forward.

Those Chamber members who had left the meeting to find the scriptwriters, huddled at the end of the terrace. Ed and Benny stood at the opposite end, near the French doors leading into the Tavern Bar. Benny's head was lowered and he snapped his fingers over and over again. Ed couldn't keep still, either. He stood on one foot, jiggled in place, then leaned against the stone wall and pushed his shoulders up and down.

Marge began to speak in a level, matter-of-fact way. "Adela was sitting right next to him." She pointed to an overturned chair by the glass-topped table. "Her hat in his face like she usually does and she was going on and on about this idea she had for a sitcom. Doreen was sittin' opposite"—she swung her chin to Mort Carmody's right—"in that chair there, and Benny was kind of wandering around the gardens, doin' his best to ignore them all. Mort kept calling him back: 'Hey, Ben, what do you think?' That kind of stuff." Marge sniffed. "If anyone were going to get poisoned, I would have bet on Adela. She was driving those guys crazy. Anyhow, you must have told everyone in the

Chamber meeting to come out here." Her little turret eyes swiveled, met Quill's, then swiveled away again. "And all of a sudden everyone was crowding around these two. A couple of people backed Benny into those rosebushes over there." She scowled suddenly. "What happened to those rosebushes over there? I took 'em out of that stupid pool and put 'em back here!"

"I put them back," Quill said firmly. "So then what happened?"

"To Mort? Well, he was goin' on about focal points or some damn thing, which was just to shut Adela up if you ask me. He got up, walked over to the buffet table, and poured himself more orange juice. Then he turned his back to put the gin in, of course, took a swig of the juice, came back here, sat down, and died."

Quill blinked. "There must be more to it than that."

"What?" Marge said irritably. "He died. D-I-E-D. Kaput. Zink." She drew a forefinger across her throat.

"Zink?"

"Zink."

Quill glanced at Marge. Her mouth was set, her teeth clenched. Fine wrinkles spanned her forehead. "Let's sit down," Quill said softly. "Come on. Right here on the grass. We can lean against the wall." She guided Marge by the elbow to the shade of the building, then gently settled her on the ground.

"I've seen worse," Marge said flatly.

Quill doubted it, but she didn't say so. "Don't look at him. It's a lot easier if you don't look."

"Huhn!" But Quill noticed she stared past the corpse, not at it. The EMTs had arrived, and they were bustling around the body. "Anyways, he choked, first, like when you swallow your own spit by mistake. Then he whooped, like something was stuck. And he turned blue. So I did the Heimlich." Marge's eyes began to blink very fast, although her expression didn't change at all. "Grabbed him from behind, made a fist, and shoved up!" She jerked her clasped hands upward. The sudden movement made Quill jump. "He was shoutin' by then. Barking, like. Adela was shouting, too. Doreen put her arm on my shoulders and said to do it again. So I did it again." She held her eyes wide open. A tear slid down her cheek. "I felt him go, you know. It's the damnedest thing. All of a sudden he was just . . . meat. Like when you skin a deer. Dead meat underneath. Loose skin on the top."

Quill put her arm around Marge's chunky shoulders.

"Anyways, there it is. It musta been poison."

"What makes you think it was poison? I mean, it could have been a heart attack. Or he could have suffocated from choking on something, Marge."

The older woman shook her head. "Hadn't had a thing to eat. And I checked."

"You mean you looked in his throat?"

"Sure. They tell ya to stick your finger down there if the food or whatever isn't going to come out, and the poor slob was dying, for chrissakes, so yeah, I stuck my finger down there. Stuck my whole goddamn hand down there, didn't I? Nothing. Not a thing."

"Then it could have been a heart attack," Quill said. "He's awfully blue, Marge."

"Yeah." She got up and dusted her chinos with brisk slaps of her hand. "And if it was a heart attack, I didn't do much of a favor by thumping his chest like I did, now, did I?"

"You can't give someone a heart attack by administering the Hiemlich," Quill said sturdily, although she had no idea if this was true or not. "That is absolutely true, Marge."

"What do you know about it?" The tears were running down her cheeks. Quill's own eyes smarted in sympathy.

"I know a lot about it. I'm an artist, Marge. I've taken tons of anatomy courses. The sternum's in the way."

"The what?"

"The sternum." Quill got to her feet and thumped her chest. "This thick bone right here. Above your, um, bosom. A human being doesn't have enough force to whack a heart through the sternum."

Marge refused to wipe her cheeks dry. Quill took a Kleenex from her pocket and dabbed at her face. Marge submitted to this as if it wasn't happening at all.

"Isn't this a charming little scene," someone said in a sneering tone.

Quill spun around. "Trooper Harris," she said flatly. "How good to see you again."

"Captain," he said briefly. "It's Captain Harris now, Miss Quilliam. And I see you're still collecting bodies."

Quill decided, quite irrationally, that she didn't like men with bullet heads and brush cuts. Harris had flat brown eyes and a mouth like a paper cut. She didn't like that about him either. "Where's my housekeeper?" she demanded.

"Detained for questioning, not that it's any of your business." His eyes wandered over her breasts and hips. "We're taking over that big room off the foyer for the investigation. The conference room. I want you in there. Now. And where's that ex-con you call your business manager? I want to talk to him, too."

Marge muttered, "Jerk."

Quill folded her arms over her chest to keep from smacking Harris on the ear. "Do you smoke cigars, Captain?"

"Do I what?"

"Studies show," Quill said, "that seventy-two percent of the people who smoke cigars do it because they know how annoying it is to other people. I think this is the secret to the universe. Some of the people in it exist to make other people miserable."

Harris shook his head, as if to get rid of flies.

"We don't try to understand Quill, you know, we just appreciate her for what she is." Howie Murchinson eased himself next to Quill and saluted Marge with a nod. Quill was very glad to see him. Hemlock Falls's best (and only) attorney-at-law was a genial man in his middle fifties. His hair was gray and thinning, and he carried a comfortable paunch. Howie was notorious for his baggy pants, ten-year-old loafers, and ancient sport coats; Meg maintained that he always looked like an unmade bed to disguise his ferocious intelligence. Doreen—who'd had four husbands and a consequent distrust of the genus *avocat*—said he looked like a slob so you couldn't argue that his high fees supported a cushy lifestyle. Quill just liked him. She gave him a brilliant smile. Howie smiled back, stuffed his hands in the pockets of his ill-fitting chinos, and rocked back on his heels. "So, Harris. What happened here?"

"Second body in two days, counselor. Doesn't look good to me. Does it look good to you?"

Howie shrugged. "Accidents happen, Harris. Do you have any idea what killed Carmody?"

All of them looked toward the body. The forensics team had finished with the photos and erected a ten-foot barricade of yellow tape around the chair, where Mort still slumped, faceup to the sun. A lab tech had already bagged his hands and feet. The empty orange-juice glass was gone, and so was the collection of carafes, plates, and glasses from the buffet table. Marge made a muffled noise and stamped off in the direction of the Inn. Harris slipped on a pair of mirrored sunglasses, which made him look so much like a stereotypical bad cop Quill wanted to clout him again. "EMT just said he's dead. But we won't know for sure until the coroner gets here. And until he does, Carmody isn't even dead, officially."

Flies were beginning to collect around the body. A small breeze brought the odor of death. "Let's move inside, out of the heat," Howie suggested.

They went through the French doors to the bar. It was filled with as many people as it had been the day before. Nate had appeared from somewhere and was serving coffee and iced tea. Howie bent to her ear. "Where is John?"

Quill's temper flared. "He's in Syracuse. It's bad

enough that Harris suspects him automatically every time some—"

"Easy, easy." He put his hand on her arm. "You're shaking, Quill. Sit down. Have you had anything to eat this morning?"

"I'm fine. And I don't want anyone to offer me anything to eat ever again!" Quill sat at a table on the edge of the group. Conversation was subdued. Adela was collapsed in a chair, chubby legs extended. The mayor fanned her anxiously with a napkin. Doreen worked behind the bar next to Nate. Quill could feel her glower. Harris walked over to a trooper standing by the arch to the hall. Both men moved aside when Everett Bland strolled in.

Quill groaned. "That's all we need!"

"Who is he?" Howie grinned. "Wait. Don't tell me. I've seen that artfully tanned face before. But where?"

"*The Jerry Springer Show*, probably," Quill said crossly. "It's Everett Bland. Strickland's lawyer. Or more accurately, the lawyer for Strickland's estate."

Bland took a cup of coffee from Doreen and came to their table. "You were right, Quill. The view from two-seventeen is spectacular."

"You're staying at the Inn?" Howie asked.

"And you are?" Bland raised his eyebrows.

"Murchinson."

"Mr. Murchinson represents us," Quill said. "Unless you can't, Howie."

"Why couldn't I?"

"Well, there's Max. Isn't that a conflict of interest?"

"Wouldn't want a conflict of interest, counselor,"

Bland said. "Even in the hinterlands that's against the canon of ethics."

"Max is a dog," Howie said dryly. "Are you here for a specific purpose, Bland?"

"Might be. At the very least we've got a cause of action for two wrongful deaths. I always like a nice civil suit." His glance appraised the long mahogany bar, the slate floor, then came to rest on the acrylics on the wall.

"We don't have any money," Quill said. She suddenly was very tired. She wanted nothing more than to put her head down and go to sleep. And it wasn't even lunchtime yet.

"You're Quilliam, aren't you?" Bland said.

"You know who I am."

"He means are you *that* Quilliam." Howie gestured at the acrylics.

Quill didn't paint often now. Perhaps two canvases a year. She was out of the art loop and not anxious to get back in again, content to display her work at the Inn. She had a new canvas up there, painted while she and Meg had been running the Palate Restaurant, where, she recalled with a stab of longing, she had plenty of time to do anything she wanted. The Palate had been a cakewalk compared with this. She'd captured Doreen, in shadow, against the wrought-iron fence in the back of the Palate's garden. One of her hands lay in sunlight, strong, age-spotted, and somehow tender.

"Very nice piece," Bland said. "Very nice. You don't exhibit anymore, do you, Quill? Keep it up. The less the public sees of your work, the higher the value."

"That's it, Bland? You're trolling?" Howie kept his voice light. Quill had known him for a long time. He was very angry.

Bland raised one eyebrow in an offensive way. "Let's not get hasty, counselor." He turned to Quill. "We'll talk later. Right now, I need some exercise. There don't appear to be any workout facilities here. Could there be a jogging path nearby? I suppose a gym is too much to ask."

"See that blonde woman right there?" Quill pointed in Sherri Kerri's direction. She was talking animatedly to Esther and Miriam. "She runs a gym. There are," she added reluctantly, "guest passes at the front desk. Just ask Dina."

Bland pursed his lips and wandered off again.

"He knows Horvath," Quill said as soon as he was out of earshot. "Does that mean anything?"

"Bland knows your Finn?"

"*My* Finn. He's not my Finn. But yes, he knows Horvath."

"How did that happen?"

"I have no idea. I think they met in L.A."

"Hmm."

"Don't just say 'hmm,' Howie. What am I supposed to do now? Can we go forward with this deal, with two deaths in a row here? Of course we can't. Meg and I decided last night. We have to solve this murder. Strickland's, I mean. And if Carmody turns out to have been murdered as well—we've got to solve that one, too."

"You aren't an officer of the court, Quill. You aren't

even a listed private detective. I'm afraid, as your lawyer, I'd have to advise you against any such activity."
Howie looked sympathetic, but not very.

"I'll tell you what I'm going to do about it," Quill
answered herself. "I'm going to get to the bottom of
this. Of all of this. And then it will go away and I can
run my Inn again."

"What about Max?" Howie said suddenly. "I can't
believe that you've left him in Flick Peterson's doghouse all this time, Quill. Poor dog."

"It hasn't been 'all this time.' It's been exactly
twenty-four hours." She looked at her watch. "Less
than that, even. And I went to visit him last night. You
know, Mr. Peterson likes him."

"Flick's a good guy," Howie agreed absently. "But
still. Max must be missing you terribly, Quill."

Quill shoved herself away from the table and stood
up. Howie made her feel horribly guilty. Poor Max!
"The first thing I'm going to do is get my dog back."
She sat down again. "Howie. How do I get my dog
back?"

"It'll take a fair bit of time," he murmured. "You
say Myles will be back next week?"

"What has Myles got to do with anything?"

"And John's back this afternoon. He should be able
to . . . well. It's going to take some doing to save your
dog, Quill. Certainly all of today. Very probably all of
this week. There has to be a hearing, and then the justice decides what to do with the dog."

"Can't I get him released on his own recognizance?"

Howie closed his eyes briefly. "TV lawyer shows

have a lot to answer for. No, Quill. Max is not a person."

"So he doesn't have his own recognizance?"

"Something like that. You may be able to get him released into your custody until the hearing. That depends on the justice."

"And you're the justice. So what do you decide?"

He shook his head. "Sorry, Quill. This isn't my bailiwick. You'll have to go into Ithaca to the Tompkins County courthouse and schedule a hearing."

"Why can't you decide what to do about Max?"

He gave a tired sigh. "Because our slick friend from the big city is right. If there's going to be a civil action for wrongful death—and no matter what the outcome of the murder investigation is, Quill, there's going to be a civil suit involving the Inn—I don't want to prejudice the case by appearing for both you and Max."

"So there is a conflict of interest."

"Right. It's the first time in my career that it involves a dog, though."

"Who's the person to talk to in Tompkins County?"

"Bernie Bristol."

"Bernie Bristol? Bernie Bristol! He's the second stupidest person I ever met! He's the justice that took over that year the village went bananas and kicked Myles out of office!"

"Well, it'll help that he's the second stupidest person you ever met, won't it?"

"Won't Max need a lawyer?"

"Nope. Just bring in a few character witnesses, talk to the vet—no wait, he bit the vet—just find some nice solid citizens who will swear Max is more noble than

Lassie and braver than Rin Tin Tin, and you'll be fine. There's no evidence of a dog bite, Quill. And the forensic evidence relating to Strickland's death is pretty clear. He was bashed on the head by someone or something, who or which couldn't possibly be a four-footed lop-eared . . ." He paused and made an effort to control himself. "Dog," he finished.

"You don't like Max," Quill accused him.

"I like Max just fine."

"Will you appear on his behalf?"

Howie eyed her narrowly. "You know that dog and my dahlias. He dug them up, Quill. All two hundred and fifty of them. Just before the dahlia show."

"So? You'd put his life on the line for a few lousy dahlias?"

"No. Of course not. Sure, I'll show up and attest to his friendly, nonaggressive, dahlia-chewing behavior. Take it easy, Quill." He rubbed his upper lip in a thoughtful way. "It'll take you a while, though. How long will John be in Syracuse?"

"Just for the day. I thought I mentioned that."

"And when will Myles be back?"

"What could Myles have to do with—oh!" Quill went "phuut!" in exasperation. "You want to keep me from investigating this murder, don't you?"

"Do I? Just relax. First things first. Spend tomorrow collecting those items I suggested—"

"What were they again?"

"Let's see: a letter from Dave Kiddermeister, a copy of the autopsy report, a copy of the police report, some character witnesses."

"That's a lot longer list than the first one," Quill said suspiciously.

"Better safe than sorry. Then Monday, hop on down to Ithaca and see Bernie. Ask him if Max can be released under your care, custody, and control."

"Wait." Quill pulled a pen from her pocket and scribbled frantically on a napkin. "Okay."

"And his veterinary records, so we can show he's legal for rabies."

"Are you sure I need all this?"

"Can't hurt."

"You want to keep me otherwise occupied so I won't investigate this murder. Or the other murder." She held up her hand. "Nope, nope. Don't bother to deny it . . . of course you do. Everyone always does. But . . . !" Quill turned and marched off.

"But what?" Howie called after her.

"It's not going to work!"

Character witnesses. The first thing to do would be to find a character witness. Quill wound her way through the crowd in the bar to her office door. She'd find Dina, who was probably in the kitchen, and get statements as to Max's affectionate, kindly nature. She scrabbled through her filing cabinets in search of a legal pad. There weren't any. There were several sketch pads, however, so she grabbed two, a pen, and went into the foyer. There was no one at the reception desk. The front door was closed. The main part of the Inn was silent. A hand-lettered sign posted at the foot of the main staircase in the foyer read DINING ROOM CLOSED—Dina's writing, Quill thought.

She went through the dining room and into the kitchen. Bjarne was at the sink rinsing brown rice. Quill greeted him and took a jug of sun tea from the SubZero. "No lunches today?"

"Captain Harris," Bjarne said gloomily. He was so tall, Quill had to crane her neck to look up at him. "No lunches and no dinners. I believe that Captain Harris was responding to concerns of Mr. Bland that Mr. Carmody had ingested a substance that may have been contaminated." He placed the colander of rice in a large bowl and covered it.

"So the dining room is closed closed? I mean, no dinners, either?"

Bjarne shook his head. With his pale eyes and white-blonde hair, he always reminded Quill of a depressed Ingmar Bergman. Until Meg took Bjarne on in her kitchen, Quill had been convinced there was a genetic link between a cook's love of food and a certain *joie de vivre*. Bjarne disproved that assumption.

"Well, it's probably for the best," Quill said. "We're not really open to the public anyhow, until the deal's signed, so you can take the day off, Bjarne."

He sighed heavily and shook his head. "I shall go to the mall," he said sorrowfully. "And what will you do, Quill?"

"You remember Max."

Bjarne's lip lifted, revealing a yellowing tooth. Quill didn't think this was a smile; more of a snarl. "You know he's in the pound? The place where Americans keep strayed pets. Actually, Max is in jail, Bjarne."

The chef smiled. "Ah."

"I'm going to get him out."

"Ah."

There was a very different tone to this second "ah." Quill persevered. "I need statements from Max's friends. About what a . . ." *Good dog* wasn't the right phrase. "Worthy dog he is. To convince the authorities to let him out."

"And if you do not get these statements?"

Quill cocked her head to one side, considering. What would a ruthless executive like Rupert Murdoch have done? "I will cry and cry," she said. "I'll be really sad."

"Sadness is part of life," Bjarne said.

"To a Finn, maybe," Quill said tartly. "I'll tell you what I'll do, Bjarne Bjarnson, if you don't write a nice note for Max. I'll put you in charge of the snack bar Horvath's bugging us to install. I've already got a name for it: the Elvis Presley Snack and Food Bar. You'll fry stuff in batter, Bjarne. Mushrooms. Chicken wings. Pickles. I'll make sure that snack bar has every single thing on its menu that Elvis Presley ate. Including the Crisco sandwiches."

"That's disgusting."

"And a dead dog is pitiful. I'll have no mercy. I warn you."

Bjarne held out his hand. He took the sketch pad and the pen. He wrote briefly, signed it, then returned it. She read:

Do not kill Max the dog.
My happiness depends upon it.

"Thanks, Bjarne," Quill said.

By nightfall, she had most of the documents Howie had suggested she obtain. The vet turned Max's medical records over after extracting her promise to switch vets. Davey Kiddermeister wrote an impassioned note that had only two misspellings. He turned over a copy of the police report and a note from forensics that indicated some of the cloth extracted from Max's teeth had come from a trooper's trousers. Quill hoped they were Harris's. The autopsy report was inconclusive; they were awaiting further tests.

She drove home to the Inn well after dark, coming up the long driveway to a darkened building and an empty parking lot.

There was no one there at all. It felt abandoned. Dina had gone back to Cornell, Doreen home to her husband, Meg was in New York, Myles in Seattle, and Max was in jail. The scriptwriters and Bland must have gone out for dinner.

She walked restlessly from room to room, then went outside into the gardens and paused for a long while on the flagstone terrace. The carriage house was visible from where she stood. A light was on in the office on the second floor. John was a dark shape against his computer screen. What had he found out about Bland and Strickland in Syracuse?

The air was soft and humid. The scent of late-blooming lilies drifted by. The sound of water over the Falls was a lulling rush. Quill lifted her hair off the nape of her neck. Sunday tomorrow. With the kitchen closed, she could sleep in. Doreen would be in to supervise the room cleaning.

She could spend Sunday morning as she liked. Where she liked. In John's bed, if she chose.

Quill turned and went up to bed alone.

CHAPTER 10

Sunday, Quill went to visit Max. She returned to a morning quiet on the surface, but rife with tensions. "It's why I don't like lakes," she explained to John over coffee on the terrace.

He laughed. "Okay, I'll bite on that one. Why don't you like lakes?"

"I like to look at lakes, of course, unless they're polluted, but you never know what's under the calm water."

"Lake monsters," John suggested.

"And watery booby traps." Quill looked out over the lawn. Yellow police tape still surrounded the table where Mort Carmody had died. Quill scraped her sandal across the stone. "This spot has a morbid fascination for me," she said glumly. She couldn't take her eyes off the chair where Mort had died.

"Do you think so? It's beautiful, Quill. You can't let Mort's death spoil it for you."

Quill tugged at her hair. "No news on why he died or how. Davey said the coroner's office is backed up. There was a terrible accident on the thruway. But it doesn't seem likely to me, John, that there would be two fatal accidents in a twenty-four-hour period. Especially when the two men worked closely together."

"It's possible, but not probable," he agreed. "If we assume that both are murder victims—we have to look at the big three."

"Means, motive, and opportunity. Something I picked up from Mort the day before yesterday led me to suspect a motive for Strickland's death. *Sneezer* was on the block."

"There were plans to cancel the show? That happens all the time in television, Quill, doesn't it? It'd be a motive if Mort needed the money and had no hope of other employment, I suppose. But it's weak."

"It *is* weak." Quill sipped her coffee happily, then set it on the arm of her chair. "I'm glad we agree. Mort didn't seem to have the necessary . . ."

"Emotional instability to kill."

"Exactly! *Exactly!*" She sat up in excitement. John grabbed her coffee cup and set it on the flagstones.

"I found out very little of substance about Strickland and Bland." John stretched his long legs out and put his hands behind his head. "Bland makes the news a lot, but the stories were all about the cases he's handled. Primarily civil suits, squabbles over land use, contractual issues with actors, negotiations with the Screenwriters Guild. That sort of thing. Strickland seems to have been a wunderkind. He made his mark on the industry early on."

"Mark? *Wound* is more like it." Just then Benny Gilpin shuffled through the French doors onto the terrace and slumped into the chair opposite Quill. "That is, if you're talking about Slick Strickland."

"Looks like you had a rough night," John said in a neutral tone.

"Eddie and I went down to that little bar off Main—what's its name? The Croh Bar. They were having a big going-out-of-business bash." Benny's eyes were bloodshot. Bits of scrambled egg were stuck in his gray beard. He yawned. "The broad that bought the place?"

"Marge Schmidt," Quill said.

"Yeah. She and her partner showed up about midnight. They made breakfast for us about four o'clock. We closed the place. Damn good food, too. Mort would have loved it." His lower lip protruded. "Poor Mort."

"You miss him," Quill said dryly. "Had you worked together long?"

"Four seasons with the duck."

Quill presumed this was the *Sneezer* show.

"He wasn't a member of the club," John said.

Benny's eyes shifted away, then darted back to appraise John. "You mean AA." John nodded. Quill kept silent. John had had his struggles there, and he had won. "No. No." Benny's tone was defensive. "It wasn't that big a problem for him. Or me, either. We both could handle it."

John nodded noncommittally. "Any financial problems?"

"Mort? Hell, yeah. Poor slob was always meeting broads in bars and marrying them. Hazard in the script-writing business. Chicks think you can give them a leg up in the industry, you know?"

More like a hazard in the drinking business, Quill thought. And chicks? She hadn't heard that term for a hundred years, at least. But she said instead, "Could Mort have murdered Neil?"

"Did he want to? Hell, yeah. There was a long line of people who wanted to murder Neil, from his ex-wives to the art department. Little shit had his fingers everywhere. But did he?" Benny squinted against the sunlight. "Jesus, my head hurts. Nah, Mort didn't have the balls to murder anybody. Even Slick. Although come to think of it, he did leave the bar after Neil went out for that walk. Headed in the same direction. But you must have seen him, Quill. You were out there, too."

"I fell asleep," Quill said apologetically. "I didn't see anyone. What about Mort? Did anyone have a reason to murder him?"

"Mort? Mort had a heart attack!" Benny's eyes widened in alarm.

"Did he have a bad heart?"

"How should I know? He smoked like a chimney, drank like a fish, could happen to any of us." Benny combed his beard, his fingers nervous. "Jesus. Mort. Murdered. No way."

Quill reached for her coffee cup to give herself time to assess this reaction. Carmody's death hadn't upset Benny; the idea that it might have been murder did.

The coffee was cold. "I'll take some of that," Benny said a little desperately.

"I'll get some fresh from the kitchen."

"I'll come in with you, if you don't mind. This sun's a bastard."

John came with them. In the dining room, they found an unshaven Eddie Schwartz sitting at one of the empty tables, his eyes glassy. "I've been sitting here and sitting here," he said plaintively. "Where's the waitress?"

"Didn't you see the sign, bonehead? The kitchen's still closed." Benny sat down next to him with a thud. "Eddie, boy. They think Mort was murdered."

"Murdered?" Eddie's mouth dropped open. "No shit?"

"We don't know . . ." Quill began. John closed his hand over hers in warning.

"I told him!" Eddie said. "That idiot, I warned him."

"Warned him about what?" Quill asked, her voice casual.

"We've got to blow this pop stand, Ben. I'm serious. We stick around here, we're going to get whacked, too."

"Who's going to whack you?" Quill demanded.

Benny hunched his shoulders. "Neil must have killed him."

"Neil was dead," John said.

Eddie thumped his hands on the table in excitement. "That's right, Benny! Neil was dead! See, Mort had something on Neil, and he was bound to get a little cash out of it, and I thought . . . but no. It doesn't make any sense."

"I'll get some coffee," Quill said. "You two just sit right there." She went into the kitchen and reemerged moments later with fresh orange juice, croissants, and hot coffee. Both men gulped the coffee. Quill sat down next to John and said firmly, "Blackmail."

"I wouldn't call it blackmail, exactly." Eddie bit into the croissant sullenly. "Gray mail, maybe."

"And why was Mr. Strickland a candidate for gray mail?" Quill looked at each of them in turn. "You might as well tell us. Somebody murdered Mort. And the odds are good that the same person dispatched poor Mr. Strickland. If you knew what Mort knew, it sounds to me as if you two might be next."

"Oh, God," Eddie whimpered.

"This dining room's closed." A voice interrupted nastily. "Why are you serving in here?"

Quill turned around. Captain Harris walked into the dining room. He had on his mirrored sunglasses and his blues. Quill hoped he was very hot in them. "Coffee?" she offered sweetly.

"Coffee's good," Ed said nervously. "Captain, is it true Mort was murdered?"

"Carmody? Who told you that?"

Both men looked at Quill.

Harris spat lightly. "She know something the ME doesn't? Or the coroner's office? Or his own doctor? Cause of death was a massive coronary. Brought on by the heat and the poor bastard's smoking habit. Plus, the son of a bitch was drunk. At ten-thirty in the morning."

Benny laughed. Quill knew the laugh was one of relief. Harris smiled thinly, acknowledging the good-old-boy joviality. "Yeah. Hard-living guy, Carmody. Anyway, you can open up this place again, Raintree. As long as everyone stays healthy, you can stay open."

"What about Strickland?" Quill asked. "Was his death natural, too?"

"Wound on the head killed him. It's consistent with a fall. We clear up the matter of the dog and the case is closed." He smirked in an insufferable way.

"My dog didn't do it," Quill said. She got up and left, her temper close to the boiling point. If Harris had delayed just five minutes, she could have gotten to the bottom of this. And dammit, it wasn't Max's fault.

Quill woke Monday morning unsure about how to dress to request a dog hearing, so she opted for "demure professional." Demure professional was hard when it was hot, but she put on panty hose, dug up a white blouse, and pulled on a challis skirt. She tried the French braids. They looked terrific, and she reminded herself not to tug at her hair, no matter how exasperating Bernie Bristol turned out to be. Then she dug through her bureau for cute photos of Max.

There weren't any cute photos of Max. There were photos of Max swimming in which the water running out of his jaws made him look like a rabid wolf. Doreen had snapped a picture of Max being called for a bath. From the dog's expression, it was easy to infer a lot of very bad things about Quill, his owner. Quill selected the one of Max asleep on his back. All four paws were in the air, and his tongue was sticking out.

That, Quill decided ruefully, was as cute as Max ever got.

By the time she came back downstairs, Dina had returned to her post at the reception desk and the Inn was blessedly humming along its Monday-morning routine. "Where is everyone?" Quill asked. "And sorry, did you have a good weekend?"

Dina punched the save key on her laptop. "Yes, I had a great weekend and I don't know where everyone is. The script seminar's today, so Bjarne's fussing around in the kitchen and John's out with the food broker and Doreen's in the middle of firing another housemaid and—"

"Stop," Quill said.

"I can't stop. I have one more thing to tell you. Meg called in a few seconds ago and I told her what happened and she's coming right back home."

"La Strazza won't like that," Quill said doubtfully.

"She said to tell you 'sisters forever.' "

"She did?" Quill was very pleased to hear this. "Well, if she calls again, you tell her back, 'Sisters forever!' "

"Got it. When will you be back?"

Quill glanced at her watch. It was after eight-thirty. County offices opened at nine. "Noonish, I think. It takes about twenty minutes to get to the courthouse. I'm going to try and spring Max. With any luck, we'll all be together for dinner—Meg, John, Doreen, and me."

"Just like old times," Dina said. "Does this mean I can have the day off?"

"You want the day off?"

"Thing is, Dave Kiddermeister wants to go out."

"Oh." Quill paused. "I don't suppose—"

"I know, I know. I dumped him last month, but he's so cute when he blushes, Quill . . ."

"It's not that. It's just that with Myles away, we don't really have the kind of access to information he would be perfectly willing for us to have if he were here."

Dina's eyebrows drew together. "I think I can translate that. You want me to pump Dave for any information he might have about the murder."

"Murders," Quill corrected her. "Harris is wrong. I don't care how the autopsy report reads. It's just too much of a coincidence, and Harris is too promotion happy for me to buy the accidental-causes bit. He wants those cases solved so that he'll look good."

"But Mort Carmody just keeled over in the heat, Quill. It's all over town that he had a heart attack, and I don't like pumping Dave for information."

"Of course he had a bad heart. The man was a chain-smoking drunk. God knows his liver couldn't have been in very good shape, either. But it wasn't that hot. He was sitting down, not exerting himself at all. And kaboom? I don't think so. And I don't like the word *pump*, Dina. I wouldn't," she added with a virtuous air, "want you to try to obtain information that wasn't available to the general public."

"Sure you would," Dina said sourly. "Okay, fine. Go ahead. But when my love life is totally wrecked because poor Dave thinks I've been using him like some sort of Mata Hari, it'll be all your fault!"

"I'm leaving now, Dina. This is me, leaving." She

slung her purse over her shoulder and walked out.

The Oldsmobile started on the first attempt, which was a good omen. When they were preparing their financial statements for the bank and Quill had tried to list the 1989 vehicle as an asset, even Doreen laughed herself into fits. But Quill liked the shabby old car; the scent was familiar, the velour seats were worn in just the right way, and she knew exactly when the gas tank needed to be filled even though the gauge didn't work. She and the car knew each other so well, it practically drove itself.

And it was a beautiful day for a drive. Quill settled into the driver's seat. This would be a respite, this drive to save her dog. She'd have time to think, to sort out the confusion of the past few days. She pulled a pen and notepad from her purse and laid them on the seat beside her. In a rather cheerful frame of mind, she pulled onto Route 15 for the short drive to Ithaca. She drove with her left hand and wrote with her right:

1. Rescue Max.

2. Neil Strickland: murder or accident? If murder, find killer.

3. Mort Carmody: murder or natural causes? If murder, find killer.

4. What was Mort's blackmail scheme? Did it involve Everett Bland? Question Ed and Benny.

5. Myles: tell him good-bye. As soon as he gets home. No chickening out.

6. Find out when and where Bland agreed to
   represent Strickland's estate.

Six impossible things before breakfast. Where had
that line come from? Quill frowned at the list.

There was a horrendous crunch. The Olds lurched
and stalled. Quill pitched forward, then back, her seat
belt cutting into her throat. Startled, she looked wildly
around, then into the rearview mirror. A huge red van
seemed to be trying to park in her backseat.

Rear-ended, dammit.

Quill unbuckled her belt and got out of the car, leaving her door ajar. Even in tourist season, there was very
little traffic on 15; it was one of the reasons she liked
the road. Aside from the van attached to her rear
bumper, there wasn't another vehicle in sight.

She hesitated a moment, waiting for the other driver
to emerge. The van was a Dodge Caravan; for some
reason, Quill remembered that this was the most popular minivan this year, driven by everyone from hot-
shot teenagers to little old ladies. The windows were
darkly tinted, and she couldn't see into the driver's
side, or through the windshield. She saw the front license plate, though. MVP 232. Peterson Motors.

There wasn't much damage to the Olds at all; the
rear bumper was shoved forward a bit. And there didn't
appear to be much damage to the van, either. The engine was running and the windshield was intact. It was
unlikely that the driver had been knocked unconscious
by the impact; it had been noisy, but slight.

Quill craned her neck and called, "Hello? Hello? Are
you all right in there?"

The van went into reverse and backed off the Olds, which settled to the macadam with a jangling thump. Quill made out a dim shape at the wheel; whoever it was was tall, or sitting on several volumes of the *Oxford English Dictionary*.

"Are you okay?"

The van shot forward. Quill leaped back, falling through the open car door onto the driver's seat. Her right heel caught on the door frame; her left leg slid forward. She shut her eyes and recoiled. There was a slap of wind. A huge dull pressure on her left foot. And the van was gone, speeding down the road.

Quill struggled to sit up. Her left foot was numb. She looked at it, bewildered. Her sandal was torn. Blood oozed from her toes.

"Yikes," she muttered. Clutching the door frame, she eased herself upright. The foot took her weight despite that curious numbness. She wriggled her toes carefully. There was a definite glitch between the intent and the result. Her toes wriggled in slo-mo, like an instant replay of a bad call in football. She limped around the Olds and checked the rear end. A nice dent, with a scrape of red paint, but that was all. She sniffed the air. No scent of gas or oil. She returned to the driver's door and bent over to look at the undercarriage. Her head swam and her vision darkened. She bent over, trying to control the urge to throw up. The sound of a car coming from behind sent a jolt of fear through her. The car stopped. Quill fumbled for her purse. There was a nail file in there. Or maybe her keys. She'd read somewhere that you could defend yourself with keys.

"Quill? Miss Quilliam?" She knew that voice: Ev-

erett Bland. Firm hands held her shoulders. Quill
caught a whiff of expensive aftershave. "Can you stand
up?"

Quill backed out of the car and straightened up in
the sunlight. "I just need a second. Thanks." The sick
feeling in her stomach ebbed, and her vision cleared.

"Are you all right?" Bland's face wore an expression
of professional concern: shrewd, a little remote, de-
tached. His cell phone stuck out of his suit-coat pocket.
For some reason, the very normality of his appearance
reassured Quill, as nothing else would have.

"I think so."

"Your foot's bleeding."

Quill looked at it and her head swam again. "It sure
is."

"Sit down for a moment." He eased her into the
driver's seat. "What happened?"

"I'm not sure. I was rear-ended by a red van." She
stopped, concentrating. She'd seen a red van not long
ago, in other circumstances.

"Miss Quilliam?"

"Yes. Sorry. I was woolgathering. I think it was a
Dodge Caravan. We both stopped. I got out, intending
to talk to the driver, and he ran over my foot."

"He?"

"You know, Mr. Bland, I'm not sure. The windows
were the tinted kind, and I couldn't see who was driving."

"And I don't suppose you had a chance to get a look
at the license plates."

Quill nodded her head. Bland whipped out his cell

phone. "We'll call the state police. You ought to report this."

"No, I'd prefer not to."

One eyebrow went up. "Why not?"

"There's very little damage to the Oldsmobile. And an accident report would just be a nuisance. I don't have time to go through all the rigmarole. And the chances of the van being found are pretty remote, wouldn't you say?"

He shrugged.

"Besides, Harris is in charge of Tompkins County now that Myles McHale is out of town, and I just . . ." She hesitated. "I just don't want to deal with him right now."

"Fine by me." He looked at her foot. The bleeding had stopped. It hurt like the devil, and the toes were puffing up. "I suppose we should get you to an ER. They do have emergency rooms in the hinterlands, don't they?"

"Of course they do," Quill said crossly. "Cornell University is about ten minutes from here, Mr. Bland. We are not exactly hillbillies, you know."

"Couldn't prove it by me." He grinned, his teeth very white in his tanned face. "No smog, no civilization."

"Funny," Quill said. "I'll be fine. Nothing's broken; it's just scraped and bruised. And you can't set broken toes anyhow. They'd clean it up and sock my insurance company with a huge bill."

"Hey," he said, "that's what the system's for."

"I'm fine, really. It was just a bump. I appreciate your stopping, though. Where are you headed?"

"Just out for a drive. Thought I might meet a few people."

Quill eyed him. "Are you filing another stay-of-business order or whatever it is?"

"No. I've got clerks to do that. Just wanted to get the lay of the land."

I'll bet, Quill thought darkly. Find out who's bribable, that's what he's doing. Aloud she said, "There won't be too many people around this early, Mr. Bland."

"Thank you for the warning."

"You're welcome," Quill said stiffly. She settled cautiously back into the driver's seat and snapped on her seat belt.

Bland stuck his head inside. His breath smelled of peppermints and his face of suntan lotion. "You're certain you're capable of driving?"

Quill turned on the ignition and revved the accelerator.

"I see that you are." He backed off and showed her a piece of paper in his hand. "You might not want to leave without this. It is your list, isn't it? Must have fallen onto the pavement when you got out of the car." Quill reached for it. Bland backed up a little more. "You interest me, Miss Quilliam. Most people write lists reminding themselves to pick up the dry cleaning, two gallons of milk, and six cartons of yogurt." He dropped it into her lap. "I'd take better care of myself if I were you, Miss Quilliam. I truly would."

"You didn't mean that to sound threatening," Quill said.

He smiled and closed the door. "I'll follow you into

Ithaca, just to see if you're going to do the ladylike thing and faint. You should take steps to avoid any more accidents, Miss Quilliam."

Quill jerked the Olds into drive and accelerated. She watched Bland in the rearview mirror. He was driving a white Taurus, the same rental car he'd registered when he'd checked in to the Inn. Quill kept to a careful speed. Her foot throbbed, but it was bearable. Her heart was beating at a normal pace, and her sudden fear was gone. "What I am," she muttered to herself, "is damn mad. And that van, Mr. Bland, was no accident." She remembered where she'd seen it now. Outside Sherri Kerri's gym the day she'd been kissing her boyfriend.

CHAPTER 11

As she had hoped, Monday morning was a quiet day at the Tompkins County courthouse. It was notoriously difficult to park in Ithaca, even during the summer months when the university town was relatively free of undergrads. Quill parked in the horrendously expensive municipal lot and limped her way down the street to the main entrance of the court house. Normally she liked Ithaca. The town was built on a series of drumlins and, as in the village of Hemlock Falls, the streets were steep and hilly, giving the town a European air. But today the climb to the county buildings was painful. And it was hot. By the time she reached the stone steps and the huge front doors, she was sweaty, her French braids were in hot coils over her shoulders, and her injured toes were pounding like the kettledrums at the end of the *1812* Overture.

It wasn't air-conditioned inside. Quill fanned herself with her list and scanned the directional board on the wall. The clerk of justice court was on the second floor. She took the elevator up, knocked briefly on the frosted glass of the door, and went in.

A waist-high counter separated the entrance from the secretarial area. In the back, Quill saw a half-open office door labeled ITHACA TOWN JUSTICE in brass letters and a melamine sign below it that read THE HONORABLE BERNARD BRISTOL. The secretarial area was empty of human beings, except for a wispy, gray-haired woman sitting at a computer console. She looked up as Quill came in. She was thin to the point of emaciation. Her wire-rimmed glasses distorted faded blue eyes. She was wearing a pink fuzzy sweater and a print dress.

"May I help you?" She had a high, nervous voice.

"Yes," Quill said. "At least I hope so. I'm Sarah Quilliam."

"Who?"

"Sarah Quilliam!" Quill said, very loudly. "I'm here about my dog."

"The animal shelter is two miles outside of town."

"No, I mean yes, he's in an animal shelter, and I want him to come home. Desperately. But Judge Bristol has to agree to let him out first."

The half-open door to Judge Bristol's office slammed shut.

"His Honor is in chambers," the wispy woman said primly.

"Miss . . . um . . . could I ask your name?"

"Mildred," she said reluctantly.

"Mildred. Could you ask him to come out of chambers, please?"

"One moment." Carefully, Mildred tapped the save key on her computer. Then she looked at Quill. She hit the shut-down key and waited until the screen went dark. Then she took her purse from underneath her desk, combed her hair, applied a layer of bright red lipstick to her mouth, and coughed delicately into a Kleenex. Finally she got up and tapped at Bernie Bristol's door, like a mouse scratching.

Quill's foot hurt. She sat down on the sagging Naugahyde couch thoughtfully provided for visitors to the Ithaca town justice. This provision, she decided, must have occurred around 1952. She looked at her foot. More blood was oozing from the toe of her damaged sandal. She took a tissue out of her purse and dabbed futilely at it. She was going to lose her toenail, that was certain.

"Ahem," Mildred said.

Quill looked up expectantly.

"His Honor would like to know if you are *that* Sarah Quilliam from Hemlock Falls."

Quill had been afraid of this. Her last meeting with Judge Bristol had gone badly. So badly, in fact, that she'd ended up in the slam for a few days. The fact that this occurred because ex-U.S. Senator Alphonse Santini had bribed him to do it didn't argue Judge Bristol's ability to overlook her felony record. Mr. Bristol was a very stupid man. Quill sighed heavily. "Yes. I am *that* Sarah Quilliam. Please tell Mr. Bristol all is forgiven. Especially if he can help me out now."

Mildred pursed her lips in a disapproving way. She

disappeared inside the justice's office again. Quill dabbed at her neck with the tissue. The cool spell in August was definitely over and done with. It had to be well over ninety in this building.

"The judge will see you in a moment," Mildred said, returning.

Quill got up.

"Wait!" Mildred commanded. She picked up the phone, tapped in two digits, and waited patiently. "Now," she said into the phone. "His office." Then she hung up.

Quill blinked at her. "Now?"

"One moment, please."

Quill sank back in the couch and opened her purse. She had a copy of the original complaint against Max, sworn out by Benny. And a handwritten letter from Dave Kiddermeister indicating that Max had not heretofore shown aggressive tendencies. There was Max's rabies certificate, his health records, and the preliminary autopsy report stating that while Neil Strickland's cause of death was under investigation, it was not the result of a dog bite.

And of course, the only picture of Max she had that showed him in a somewhat positive light.

Quill looked at the picture and smiled a little. Aggressive dogs didn't sleep on their backs with their vulnerable underbellies exposed.

The glass front door opened and shut again. A security guard walked in. He had a good start on a potbelly and was in sore need of some dandruff shampoo. He glanced at Quill and away again. He hooked his thumbs in his belt and hitched up his pants. A .38 was holstered at his back. Quill hoped the safety was on.

Mildred squeaked, "His Honor will see you now."

"Thank you." Quill got up and limped to the counter. Mildred opened the gate for her, and she walked in, the security guard right behind her. He followed her all the way to Bristol's office, then wedged himself in a corner.

"Miss Quilliam," Justice Bristol said.

"Your honor,"·Quill said. She smiled. Bernie Bristol drove her nuts. He seemed blissfully unaware that his status as justice—an office open to any civic-minded citizen who chose to run for it—was not the same as the justice of the state supreme court. Or the Supreme Court of the United States, for that matter. Bernie was a retired engineer from Xerox who grasped, dimly, that there was a difference between judges and justices, but not much. He was short, perhaps five-six, with a pointy sort of head and an expression eerily similar to the nodding toy dogs often found on the dashboards of '65 Impalas. "Sorry to bother you so early in the morning."

"Extended office hours were my idea," he said. "The courts of the land should be open to any citizen in need, at any time."

"His Honor is one of the most dedicated people I know," Mildred said proudly.

"Dedicated to justice, I hope," Quill said brightly. "This shouldn't take too long, Mr. Bris—I mean Your Honor. And justice must be done," she said firmly. She dabbed at her neck again. "May I sit down?"

"How much are you bleeding?" asked Mildred severely.

"It's just my toe," Quill said, somewhat apologetically. "I stubbed it. Shouldn't be wearing sandals on pavement, I guess."

"It's all over your neck," Mildred said. "I guess she can sit down, Your Honor, but blood's one of the hardest things to get out of carpet. *Moreover*"—she swung a gimlet gaze in Quill's direction—"I don't believe a word about you stubbing your toe. I believe she assaulted someone, Your Honor."

The security guard hitched at his belt in a meaningful way.

Quill counted to ten, then said carefully, "I'm just here about a very small matter, sir. Since you've been in Hemlock Falls, I've acquired a dog."

"A dog?" Bernie looked confused.

"A poor stray dog." Quill looked sidelong at Mildred. "He was just skin and bones when I found him, sir, and you wouldn't believe how grateful he was for the slightest kindness shown him. He was just the sweetest thing you can imagine. Why, if I don't let him curl up at the foot of my bed at night, he cries in the most affecting way."

Mildred wasn't buying this. Bernie, on the other hand, looked a little wistful. "My wife won't let me have a dog," he said to no one in particular. "What's his name?"

"Max," Quill said. "And I miss him very much. Well, you know that we run an inn, my sister and I. And we had some guests come from L.A. a few days ago. Slick, oily, city folk."

Mildred shook her head. "Tsk-tsk-tsk."

"And one of them was a TV producer. I think," Quill added mendaciously, "he directed one of those Jerry

Springer–type shows where they get those poor people on and torment them into beating each other up."

"I seen it," the security guard said. "I seen that one. Terrible. Just terrible."

"It is indeed," Mildred said.

"This guy, Neil Strickland, attacked Max with my umbrella."

"Huh!" said the security guard. "It just goes to show. Killed the poor dog, did he?"

"Oh, no. But Max defended himself. He jumped on the guy and made him drop the umbrella."

"Bit him something awful, I guess," said the guard. "Lotta blood and that?"

"Max didn't touch him," Quill said impressively. "I have the autopsy report right here."

"Max killed the guy?" Bernie Bristol asked.

"No-no-no-no! The guy died from something else. Something else entirely. And at a different time entirely. But poor Max got caught up in the whole thing." Quill waved her hand vaguely. "And his friends—the guy's friends, I mean—took their revenge out on Max. Here! Would you like to see his picture? You couldn't ask for a nicer dog than Maxie." She proffered the photo of the sleeping Max to Benny. The guard peered over her shoulder. "That dog's dead," he said.

"No, he's not dead. He sleeps like that."

The guard shook his head. "I know a dead dog when I see one. I don't know no dogs that sleep on their backs with their bellies turned up. Ain't natural."

"It is when you're as inoffensive and gentle as Max is." Quill shoved the picture back in her purse. "And of course, there was more stupid trouble. The lawyers got involved. And you know how they can mess things up." She glanced hastily at Bernie. She'd been right. Bernie didn't like lawyers much. She figured lawyers didn't like Bernie much, either. "So. All I need from you, sir, is an order to let poor Max out of the pound until his hearing comes up."

"Dangerous-dog hearing," Mildred said, confirming Quill's impression that Mildred really ran this office. "Form 62.1a. Requires just your signature, Your Honor." She leveled that fierce gaze at Quill again. "Do you have any documents attesting to his character?"

"As a matter of fact I do," Quill said a little smugly. "From one of our deputies, no less."

"Not the one you're sleeping with," Mildred said tartly. She permitted herself a small smile. "Oh, yes. I've heard about you, Miss Quilliam."

Quill hoped her grin didn't look as ferocious as it felt. "Not that one. A totally disinterested party." She gave them Davey's statement, then the rabies certificate, and finally the health records from the vet.

"I don't see why we can't do this, Mildred," Bernie Bristol said. "Is there a reason why we can't do this?"

Mildred pinched her upper lip between her thumb and forefinger. "Only problem I can see is if he kills someone else."

"He didn't kill anyone!" Quill said.

"Well, if he attacks someone else, then, because you admitted yourself, Miss Quilliam, that the dog did lunge at Mr. Strickland."

"He lunged at the umbrella. I believe," Quill added thoughtfully, "that someone must have beaten Max with an umbrella when he was a puppy."

"Aw," said the guard.

"Aw, indeed."

"Your Honor undoubtedly wishes to remand the poor doggie to Miss Quilliam's custody under certain circumstances," Mildred said.

"Yeah?" Bernie said.

"And those circumstances would be?" Quill asked brightly.

"Confined to the Inn and its grounds. No access to the guests. Leashed at all times when not under your direct supervision."

"For how long?" Quill asked.

"Until the dangerous-dog hearing." Mildred reached across Bernie's desk, took the gavel, and whacked it smartly on the desktop. "We'll schedule that as soon as the results of Neil Strickland's autopsy are complete."

"Suits me," said the guard.

"And you, Miss Quilliam?" Mildred demanded.

"Thank you," Quill said. "Thank you very much."

"Then the doggie's free. Unless, of course, he does something else." Mildred looked at Quill over her wire-rimmed glasses. "I trust that there will be no further incidents of any kind?'

"Never," Quill said. "I absolutely promise."

If her toes hadn't been so sore, Quill would have skipped out of the county courthouse. As it was, she hobbled out of the elevator, with Max's release order folded carefully in the pocket of her challis skirt.

"Ah, Miss Quilliam. Decide to notify the sheriff's office after all?" Everett Bland rounded the corner and stopped in front of the elevator. Quill looked past him;

an arrow pointed down the hall under a sign that read
DEEDS AND ESTATES.

"Mr. Bland," Quill said. He wasn't sweating in the
heat, Quill noticed crossly. "Checking on the assessed
value of my inn, by any chance?"

"Hmm?"

"Look, I don't know why you're wasting your time
with us, Mr. Bland. You've got a reputation for dealing
with the high rollers, the money guys"—she waved her
hands—"the moguls? Why are you—" She stopped in
mid-flow. She could almost hear Meg's voice in her
head: Well, duh!

Who else but Bland could be behind the deaths?
Mort knew he wasn't Strickland's lawyer when Strickland had been alive. What else had Mort known before
he had been shut up for good?

"Sorry." She smiled. "It's the heat. There's a saying
out here in the hinterlands, Mr. Bland. A man's gotta
do what a man's gotta do. So I'm not going to ask you
a thing about why you're looking into our financial
worth. Would you"—she batted her eyelashes—"like
to take me to lunch?"

"Here?"

"Oh, Ithaca has a lot of wonderful little restaurants.
We'll go to Tapas."

"It's a little early for me, Miss Quilliam. And I need
to make a stop at the university first. And I have a
plane to catch at three o'clock. I've got to make a short
trip to Chicago."

"We'll miss you," she said.

"You won't miss me for long. I'll be back tomorrow
evening."

"I'll be happy to take you to Cornell. Ithaca can be a bit confusing."

Bland nodded thoughtfully. "All right. Then we'll go to Tapas?"

"Yes," Quill said recklessly. "And I'll buy."

The day was a waste. Bland picked up some maps from Cornell, told some very amusing stories at lunch, and Quill was no further along in her investigation than she had been at the very beginning.

Bland dropped her off at the municipal parking lot. She went back to the Olds, paid the exorbitant parking fee, and swung back onto Route 15 to go home with a sense of satisfaction tempered by annoyance. She could cross off item one on her list—Max—and go on to the second.

What had Neil Strickland done? And why was it worth two deaths?

Route 15 held a small amount of Monday-afternoon tourist traffic. The Finger Lakes had been a significant tourist attraction since the mid-nineteenth century. And with the flourishing boutique winery trade, more and more people were coming from out of state to spend the summer months in upstate New York. The miles wore on. Quill's foot throbbed. The air conditioning in the Olds was iffy at best, and the hotter she became, the more certain she was that the red minivan was out to get her.

Most of the tourists on the road drove vans.

None of the vans she saw, though, were red, late model, or had dented front fenders with scrapings of black paint. Quill swerved to avoid a little old couple driving their Taurus at thirty miles an hour. She narrowly missed an Escort coming in the opposite direction. She pulled back into the northbound lane short of breath, her heart pounding. She was behaving like an idiot. The red van had rear-ended her by accident. What had she been doing at the time she'd been hit?

Writing her investigation list. Quill glanced at the passenger seat, reached over to the spot where the list had lain, pretending to hold a pencil.

A car horn nearly blasted her out of her seat. A Trans Am whizzed by her window, the horn sounded again, and an irate male voice shouted, "Fer chrissakes, lady! Watch where'n the hell you're going!"

Quill raised her hand in timid apology. Perhaps she had inadvertently braked when she was writing her list? Or drifted over the shoulder? And maybe Everett Bland's appearance had been totally accidental; Route 15 was the main road to Ithaca, and you had to have lived in Tompkins County for a long time to be able to navigate the back roads to Ithaca and not get lost. "Well, the jury's out," she muttered aloud. Then a little guiltily, she fished her list out of her purse and read the second item. Results of autopsy report on Neil Strickland. Surely Andy Bishop would have a better idea of how Strickland died. Quill knew he wasn't with Meg in New York. If she stopped to see him, she could get her toes cleaned up before Doreen saw her foot and pitched one of her notorious hissy fits.

Andy had a small office for private patients attached to the Hemlock Falls Clinic. Quill pulled into the parking lot and noted with relief that his Jeep Cherokee was still there. She limped into his waiting room and greeted Nadine Peterson with a grimace.

The receptionist raised her eyebrows. "My God, what happened to you?"

"It's just my foot," Quill explained. "My toes got run over."

"By what?"

Quill waved rather vaguely. "Andy's still here?"

"He's just finishing up with his last patient." Nadine's eyes flew to the wall clock. It was after five. "I thought I was going to get home on time tonight, but I guess not."

"I'm sorry, Nadine."

Nadine, a busty bottle blonde, had been widowed several years before, and her husband, Gil the car dealer, hadn't left her much money. She'd packed up and gone to Syracuse for a while, then returned to Hemlock Falls, where, she claimed, life was a lot less of a hassle than in the big city. "No help for it, I guess," she said cheerfully. "And it's not like I have a date tonight or anything. Besides, I might be laid off soon, anyway. Might as well get the time in."

"You mean, because Andy's moving to New York?" Quill said. She hadn't thought about the effect of Andy's move to New York on Hemlock Falls. "Is someone coming in to take over the practice?"

"Oh, yeah." Nadine's weary blue eyes got a little brighter. "Haven't you heard? Andy got a great offer from a group out of Buffalo. We're going to have six doctors at least."

"Six? How can we support six doctors?"

"Well, they don't all have the same specialty, of

course. There's a GYN, and a pediatrician, a cardiologist, like that."

"My goodness." Quill eased herself down onto a chair. "You'll be able to work for them, I'm sure."

"We'll see. You know, you look terrible," Nadine said frankly. She snapped her gum. "You sure it's just your foot that's banged up? Looks like someone tried to cut your throat."

Quill brushed at the dried blood on her neck. "Must have come from the Kleenex."

"Well, don't just sit there, honey. Get into the examining room and I'll get Dr. Bishop."

"Okay. Nadine?"

"Yeah."

"Who took over Gil's dealership after ... um ..."

"One of his cousins. Frankie. Why?"

"Does he still rent cars to tourists?"

"Sure does. Makes a good buck, I think, although he sure doesn't give any of it to me. Now, get on in there, Quill, before your foot falls off entirely."

Quill limped meekly into the small room where Andy, at one time or another, had examined most of Hemlock Falls. She hoisted herself onto the examining table and looked at her foot.

"Wow!" Andy entered with his usual air of quiet competence. "The game's clearly afoot, Watson. Glad it wasn't a head."

"Very funny."

He pulled up the rolling stool and sat in front of her. Gently he removed her sandal. Quill looked down at his neatly parted blond hair. He was short, not much taller than Meg, and weighed perhaps forty pounds more than her sister—who'd never topped a hundred pounds in her life. Quill liked him a lot, but found him colorless compared with Myles and John. She suspected that her volatile sister loved him for his calmness and reticence.

"So how did this happen?" He bent her toes back and forth. "Wiggle them, please."

Andy had less tolerance for Quill's investigative activities than Myles did; he became even grimmer and quieter when they involved Meg. But she didn't know for certain that the red minivan had intended to push her off the road (or worse). As a matter of fact, the more she thought about it, the less certain she was that the car crash was intentional. "I went to Ithaca this morning to see about springing Max from the pound. I got into a fender bender, and when I got out of the Olds to look at the damage, the guy took off. But not before he ran over my foot."

"You're kidding!"

"The car's fine. I'm fine."

"At least one toe's broken. But we'll take an Xray, just to be certain." He got up. "You're pretty sure this had nothing to do with the—ah—events at the Inn the past few days?"

"I don't see how it could," Quill said honestly. Which was true. She didn't see much of anything yet about this case. If it was a case.

Andy beckoned. She hopped off the table and followed him into the small shielded area holding the radiology equipment. She flexed her foot according to instructions and waited until he'd shoved the frame into the developer before she asked about Neil Strickland's autopsy results.

"It's very strange," Andy responded. "I talked with the Tompkins County coroner. She's seen a spinal injury like it once before, when she was a resident at Bellevue. They brought in a boxer who'd sustained a concussion as a result of an upper cut." He demonstrated in an absentminded way. His right fist thrust up and stopped under an imaginary chin. "This guy Strickland's spine was broken clear through at C-1 and C-2. He was healthy, young, his bones were strong. She couldn't imagine a human being packing enough of a wallop to take his head off. Which is literally what happened."

"Ugh."

"Anyway, it's the fracture that killed him. Severed the spinal cord, shoved the top vertebra into the medulla, and bingo. He must have dropped like a stone. The cut on the posterior part of the skull was sustained when Strickland fell backward after he was killed."

"So Max didn't do it."

"Max is in the clear." The timer beeped on the developer and Andy withdrew the film and held it up to the ceiling light. "Now, you, Meg's sister, have a nice fracture of the first, second, and third metatarsals. Ouch. I wouldn't normally cast a toe fracture, but in your case, I'm going to make an exception. It's a walking cast for you, my girl."

"Casts are hot. And itchy."

"It's either that or stay off your feet for three weeks."

"Okay," Quill said reluctantly.

"You wait right here. I'm going to send Nadine home, then come in and do it myself."

"You are a peach."

"Meg's train isn't due in until six-thirty. So I've got time to kill. Can you hobble back to the examining room? I'll be back in a few minutes."

Quill resettled herself on the examining table and contemplated her toes. The last time she had broken a bone, she was thirteen. She and Meg were taking horseback-riding lessons, and she'd pitched over a fence when the gelding she was riding refused to jump. The cast on her arm had driven her crazy.

Andy returned with a stainless-steel bucket and a roll of plastic stuff. She was grateful to discover that cast technology seemed to have advanced a lot in twenty-three years; the procedure was quick and the cast light. Andy made Quill sit with her foot elevated for twenty minutes while the stuff dried, then she took a few experimental steps. "I can walk with this! Thanks!"

"Just don't go running any marathons. And no chasing crooks either, okay?"

"I'm glad you and Meg finally set a date."

He smiled a little. "Are you?"

"Well, sure. She deserves to be happy."

"And how happy do you think she's going to be living with me in New York? Away from here?" Andy's face, inexpressive to begin with, became even more remote. He disposed of the extra bandages and rinsed the stainless-steel bucket in the lab sink.

"Things change," Quill said, with regret. "I never want them to. I want to be thirty-six forever, with the Inn full of paying guests with good credit and Meg singing her horrible out-of-key songs in the kitchen. But that doesn't say anything about what Meg wants. She wouldn't move to New York with you if she didn't want to, Andy."

"I hope not."

"What do you mean?"

He shook his head and sighed. "I don't know. Just a feeling I have. It's not like her to pass up a chance to cook at La Strazza. The *Times* is supposed to show tonight, you know. They bugged out of the Saturday review."

"Nerves?" Quill suggested.

He grinned openly at that. "You know Meg's nerves. She throws things when she's anxious. She doesn't calmly hop a train back home."

"True. Well, if you don't know, Andy, I surely don't. We've been on the outs recently."

He tugged at one ear. "As a matter of fact, so have we. I'm meeting her train tonight, but she said she wanted to have dinner with you. So, Quill. If Meg says anything to you. Anything at all about our—relationship—or about the move, will you ask her to talk to me? Will you tell her that there isn't anything she can't talk over with me?"

"Of course I will, Andy. But she knows that. Meg's about as open as anyone can get."

He shook his head slightly. "I don't know. Just . . . tell her I care about her. And I want her to talk to me. Anytime."

"Sure. But I know things will be fine."

Quill, her limp refined to a hobble, had one more stop to make before she could retrieve her dog.

The same brave little pennants she recalled from years gone by still fluttered in the breeze at the Peterson dealership. Quill pulled into the lot and parked, eyeing the glass-fronted doors thoughtfully. Which of the numerous Peterson clan was Frankie? She flipped through her mental Rolodex and couldn't come up with a face. A tattoo was what came up, and she recognized it on the brawny forearm lying on the open car window: hearts, with the word *mother* entwined.

"If it isn't Miss Sarah Quilliam."

"Hello, Frank." Quill got out of the car. Like all the Peterson clan, Frankie was blond. His hair was thinning and his white short-sleeved dress shirt clung to his chest in the heat.

"You come to trade the Olds in finally?"

"I like the Olds!" Quill protested.

"That model year has a lot of trouble with the transmission. You should be looking at a nice sporty minivan, all the work you have to do at the Inn."

"It's not about minivans that I've come, Frank. Can we go inside for a minute?"

"Sure thing. I've got some coffee." He eyed her sideways as she limped to the showroom door. "What happened to you?"

"A minivan happened to me. I was out on Route 15 and this guy rear-ended me, then ran over my foot. He didn't stop. I got his license plate number, though. He bought the car from you."

The showroom was blissfully cool. Quill sank into a chair and produced her list. "The plate number's right here. It was a late model Dodge Caravan. Cherry red."

"Huh." Frank read the list, his lips moving. "You investigating again, Quill? Thought the sheriff put the kibosh on that last time. Or is it John that you're going out with . . ."

Quill grabbed the paper back, reminding herself that Hemlock Falls was a small town. "MVP 232," she said firmly. "You can ignore the other stuff on my list. It's . . . um . . . creative brainstorming. I'm writing a screenplay."

"Hey! I heard about that! Harvey Bozzel was in here earlier today talking all about it. Seems these guys from Los Angeles are up here scouting talent for TV."

"Mm," Quill said.

"You know, I have a pretty good idea for a TV show myself. Have you ever seen a show where the detective runs a car dealership? You think it might me something these L.A. guys would be interested in?"

"Well, I'm not sure."

Frankie shook his head. "I've been thinking about it a lot since Harvey was in here. I even wrote down some ideas for a couple scripts. I'd show them to you, but no offense, Quill, you never know who's going to steal a great idea. No offense."

"None taken," Quill said charitably. "About this van, Frank."

"Sure, sure. Sorry you got hurt." He shook his head again and went "tch-tch." "People these days." He walked over to a row of filing cabinets and pulled the top drawer open with a flourish. "Things have been kinda slow, lately. I haven't sold a red minivan, but I've rented one. As a matter of fact, I rented a passel of 'em. Not all red, of course. Here we go. Donovan Engineering. Rented pretty near all my stock last week."

"Donovan Engineering? Is that a local firm?"

"The credit card was out of San Diego."

"Do you have an address? And the name of the driver of the red minivan?"

"Uh." Frankie wriggled his shoulders uncomfortably. "Can't say as I have a complete driver's list. I mean, the guy wanted to rent six vehicles, Quill, and I wasn't about to nail him to the wall with all that paperwork."

"Then the company address."

Rather sheepishly, Frank handed her the address. Quill wrote it down. The name on the credit card was Simon Cranshaw. "Never heard of him," she muttered. "Nuts." She got up. "Thanks, Frank."

"No problem. You come in anytime you want to trade that Olds in, Quill. But you look a little—frazzled. You ought to go home and put that foot up."

"Have to get my dog first, Frank. And then I've got to make a few phone calls."

CHAPTER 12

"So, Max. We've made it home without getting dive-bombed by a cruise missile, broadsided by an army tank, or shot at by duck hunters."

Max whined. He sat in the front, as he liked to do, and had kept his head out the window all the way home. His coat was brushed, he'd obviously been well fed, and he smelled like herbal shampoo. Quill couldn't tell if he was happy to be home or not. She parked behind the Inn and turned off the ignition. "This whole business is creeping me out, Maxie." He whined in sympathy. "It's Bland who's behind this. It has to be. But why? And what does he want?" The dog pawed at her knee. "So we're home. Are you glad to be home?" She opened the driver's-side door. Max pushed past her with a thundering bark. Tail wagging, barks cranked to optimum decibels, he took off across the lawn and disappeared over the lip of the Gorge.

"Max!" Quill hobbled after him as fast as she could. All she saw of him was the tip of his dun-gray tail. Two men in hiking gear trudged along the riverside. One of them looked up in alarm at the barking.

"It's all right!" she shouted. "He's harmless!" Max bowled out of the brush and raced circles around the hikers, barking his fool head off. Quill resisted the impulse to shout various four-letter words and muttered them instead. The hikers waved at her. Quill hoped that their fists were merely clenched and not—oh no, a backpack lay near the water. Max grabbed it and shook it. Maps, clipboards, and what looked like instruments of various kinds tumbled onto the ground. The owner danced with rage, then bent and picked up a large stick. Max knew about sticks, but not, fortunately for the hiker, the way he knew about umbrellas. He swung the emptied backpack and let it fly. It fell into the stream, where it bobbed gently just out of reach. One hiker waded into the water. The other stormed up the Gorge toward Quill.

"The coward dies a thousand deaths, the brave man dies but one," Quill muttered. "Oh, dear." She braced herself against the Olds.

The man coming up the Gorge was in his late thirties. He was heavily tanned, with thick dark blond hair, a neatly trimmed mustache and beard, and eyes that were as blue as . . . Quill couldn't think of anything to compare them to. But he was drop-dead gorgeous. And madder than . . . again, she couldn't think of anything. But he was furious. He leaped over the stone wall that protected the parking lot from the incline below.

"Hey," he said, his face thunderous. He looked at her foot, then back up at her face and hair. "Gee, he got you, too. Are you okay?" He came closer. He was wearing jeans slung low around his lean hips, a madras shirt, and an orange hard hat. "Who *owns* that bloody hound? Have you got a dog warden around here?"

"Um," Quill said cautiously. "Not right around here, anyway." Which was true. Flick was out on Route 15, which wasn't anywhere near around here, or not very. "I'm Sarah Quilliam." She extended her hand. He shook it briefly and well. "Did your friend get his pack back?"

"That's the trouble with words like backpack. Did you get your backpack back when you lost it on the track?"

Quill burst out laughing.

"Yeah, well, I hope so. The Palm Pilot's in there and all our data for today is on it."

"Data?"

"Survey data. We've been in this area all week. Pretty place, upstate New York."

"What are you surveying?"

His face closed down. He shifted slightly away from her. "Well, our clients aren't real happy if we bruit their names about. I'm Simon Cranshaw."

"Simon Cranshaw. Simon *Cranshaw*? From Donovan Engineering?"

"Yeah. Look, I think somebody ought to do something about the dog. Do you know the people who run this place?"

Quill stared at him. This was Sherri's boyfriend. It had to be. No wonder she'd been making out with him in the gym. Quill wouldn't have wanted to wait to go upstairs either.

"Hey! Do you know who owns this dog?"

He would have recognized her. So he wasn't the one who had rear-ended her. But he'd rented five vehicles from Frankie. It must have been one of his men. Quill was gleeful at her good luck. "Yes. Yes, I know who owns the dog."

His glance rested sympathetically on the Oldsmobile. "You work here, huh? Waitress?" He didn't wait for her reply. "I've heard it's owned by a pair of crazy sisters. And of course, they had that poor slob kick off in the gorge this week, so maybe I'll just ask you to take a message to them. They've got more problems than I have."

"Did you see anything the day the man in the gorge died?" Quill asked eagerly.

His gaze flicked over her. Obviously he thought she was the kind of person who would watch shows called *The World's Most Bloody Car Crashes* for the sheer bloodiness of it. "We were on the south side of the village that day. But we saw the damn dog, of course. Look, just tell your boss, or bosses, to keep the dog tied up. All right? If they can't keep him under control, I'm going to have to call animal control."

Quill had a short debate with herself, and won. There was a code among women. You didn't flirt with other women's lovers. On the other hand, it had surely been Simon in the gym. Quill hadn't really seen his face. And she badly wanted more information about why an engineering company was tramping around Hemlock Falls. "Would you and your friend like to come in for something cold to drink? The bartender's a friend of mine. It's got to be awfully hot out here. And it's headed toward quitting time, isn't it?"

"Hey, sure! Your bosses won't mind?"

"Miss Margaret's not back from New York yet. She's the one you have to watch out for."

"What are they, geezer refugees from the nineteenth century? She makes you call her Miss Margaret?"

"She's got a temper, Miss Meg," Quill said humbly. "I'll meet you in the bar. Just follow the building around until you get to the flagstone terrace. Tell Nate that Quill said to take care of you. And your friend's name?"

"Norm."

"Great. I'll come in to see you and Norm my next break."

She slipped in the kitchen, said "hey" to Bjarne, who asked her gloomily if that was Max he'd heard barking his fool head off, and went upstairs to her room. Andy had given her a plastic bootie thing that protected the walking cast, and she took a fast, hot, and very welcome shower. She sprayed on some Tea Rose, pulled on a gauzy summer dress (it was hot! she told herself), and combed out her hair. When she limped into the Tavern Bar, she was feeling a lot better. And she was very curious about the surveying.

Something was up. Something was definitely up.

Simon sat at the bar with his back to Quill, his friend at his side. The backpack was on the floor, dripping water. Quill slid onto the stool next to Simon. "Hi, guys!"

Simon's jaw dropped.

"Glad to see you retrieved the Palm Pilot," Quill said in the tone of one who knows. She leaned across Simon in a cloud of rose-scented perfume. "Norm? Did you save the north-end data?"

Norm, a sturdy Chinese with black horn-rim glasses, looked at Simon with confusion. "I thought we weren't going to tell anyone about the resort."

Quill froze. *Resort?*

"And so you got Max out of dog jail twice," Meg said later that evening. They all sat at the kitchen prep table eating dinner, just as Quill had envisioned on her way to the Tompkins County courthouse: Doreen, John, Meg, and herself. Max lay on the slate floor near her stool, nose buried in her cast foot. He'd been brought home by an unusually cranky Davey Kiddermeister, and was in disgrace.

Meg craned her neck to look at him. "So Norm the hiker got his backpack back . . ." She blinked. "What did I just say? Anyhow, clever old you discovered somebody may be surveying unknown portions of Hemlock Falls for a resort of some type, you don't know which or what."

Quill suspected her sister of sarcasm. "I thought I had a pretty great day! Max is free. And we've got a great clue."

"What is this great clue? That somebody may—"

"Oh, shut up, Meg. Don't you see? What is it that you always say, John? Follow the money."

"It's 'show me the money,' " Doreen said. "From that movie."

Quill refused to be distracted. "Didn't you wonder

why all this high-powered lawyer was bothering with a dinky little civil suit against the Inn?"

"No!" Meg said crossly. "I'm a fairly well-known chef, you know. He would have gotten a lot of visibility suing me. Well, maybe not. But he probably wanted me to end up as his pet chef."

Doreen and Quill exchanged glances. Then they both looked under the table at Meg's feet. "Uh-oh," Doreen muttered. "Yella socks." Meg's moods could frequently be inferred from the color of the socks she wore. Yellow was not a good sign.

"But Bland is such a fool that he's not all that interested in the food," Quill said soothingly. "When people come because of you, Meggie, as they always have done and always will do, they book months in advance and they're really fussy about the menus, and they talk their way into the kitchen so they can see you cook!"

"A resort in Hemlock Falls," Doreen mused. "What kinda resort? Disney World? Like that?"

"I couldn't get any more out of them. Once Simon realized I was one of the 'crazy sisters,' he hauled Norm out of there, and his backpack, too." She took a bite of red snapper and swallowed it thoughtfully. Meg had grilled it with fresh lime and cilantro. "This is fabulous, Meg."

"Yeah," Meg said listlessly. She nudged Max with her foot. "So you're going to tackle Bland about this resort when he gets back from his trip?"

"Yep. I think we're onto something, here. I think the mysterious something that Mort had on Neil Strickland had to do with this project. I did get out of Norm that

JoyMax is their client." Quill, unsettled by Andy's question of less than two hours before, kept looking at her sister, then looking away again. Was it her imagination, or were those shadows under Meg's eyes? And was she pale beneath her summer tan? "Anyhow, money's the best motive for murder."

Meg wiggled her eyebrows. "This mysterious something that Mort may or may not have known about Strickland doesn't get us any further toward determining who killed Mort. Or why."

"Bland killed Mort," Quill said confidently. "He slipped something into his drink."

"What kind of a something?"

Quill stuck her hand into the pocket of her gauzy dress. "This!"

"That's one of Sherri's herbal powders." John took it and turned it over. " 'Vital Life Herbal, a multiple vitamin, mineral, herbal, all-vegetable food supplement.' Good grief, there's at least a hundred ingredients to this."

"They're listed alphabetically. Look under *N*."

"Nicotina flower."

"And *C*."

"Cocoa bean." John raised one eyebrow. "Nicotine and caffeine. Enough to kick off a heart attack?"

"The nicotine doesn't have an RDA dose, but the caffeine does."

"Six thousand six hundred and sixty-seven percent of the daily requirement." John whistled. "This stuff isn't regulated by the FDA."

"Not yet." Quill folded her arms and sat back. "So, I gave Davey a sample of this to send to the forensics lab in Albany. What're the odds we find it in poor Mort's bloodstream?"

"Was Bland even around when Mort was swilling gin that morning?"

"He didn't have to be. That was Mort's private supply. He could have doctored it anytime."

"And Mort killed Neil. How?" Meg demanded. "Why? All that John and I have come up with so far is stuff that substantiates this wild theory about the resort. Both men were involved with mega-real-estate deals. And JoyMax has got enough bucks to invest. And the Finns have some connection with this whole deal because Horvath was in L.A. and knows Bland. But none of this . . . this"—Meg flung her hands up in exasperation—"*marinade* of deal making has anything to do with the dead bodies."

"It's a marinade all right," Quill said in a thrilling voice, "but it's a marinade for murder!"

"Let's change the subject," Meg said flatly. "This investigation into nothing is stupid. Let's talk about Max. I think Max liked being at Flick's. How did Flick like him? He didn't offer to keep him, by any chance?"

"Forget it. Max is home. And he's learned his lesson. Haven't you, Max?" Quill bent over and ruffled the dog's ears. "He didn't *jump* the guy with the stick, you know. He ran off. Good boy."

Max groaned, yawned, and shoved his muzzle into Quill's instep.

"Reason he's got his nose stuck on your foot is that blood," Doreen said. "Never known a dog yet that didn't like the smell of blood."

Quill wiggled her toes.

"It's amazing all it is, is broke," Doreen continued

in a ruthless way. "It coulda been took right off. And as far as I'm concerned, Meg, this investigation's back on. Your sister coulda got killed, too. You sure you didn't get any part of that license number?"

Quill finished the rest of her strawberry soup and reached for a slice of carrot cake. "Not enough."

"And no idea who might have tried to run you over?" John's mouth had grim lines at the corners.

Quill shook her head. "If someone actually did try to run me over. It sounds crazy, but it may have been the way I was driving."

Doreen opened her mouth, then closed it firmly. Meg looked up at the ceiling and hummed a few bars of "The Little Old Lady from Pasadena."

"That's not funny," Quill said crossly.

Meg raised her eyebrows. "It's your driving that's funny. Honestly, Quill, I'm amazed every time you come back intact from a trip to the grocery store. It's not that you're a bad driver, it's that you're a *terrible* driver. Remember all those tickets you got when you drove the cab in New York?"

"Everybody gets tickets driving cabs in New York. And besides, nothing got dented except the bumper."

"Just your foot!"

"That wasn't a result of *my* bad driving. That was because the other guy couldn't drive. I have a lot of questions about this case that don't have a thing to do with driving skills. Why was Everett Bland following me?"

"Are you sure he was following you?" Meg asked skeptically.

"I don't know. But it's a suspicious coincidence,

don't you think? When I left the Inn, he was supposedly on his way to Sherri's gym. And he asked Dina where I was; she told me that when I went to let Max in after his little sojourn into the Gorge just now. And she told him where I was. Bland, I mean. And he left right after I did. He's got a cell phone. Did he call the driver of the red minivan? I've got other questions, too. How and when did Horvath meet Neil Strickland's lawyer? Why did the *Sneezer* people choose this particular Inn to meet at to try to rescue their show? Mort was terrified the show was going to be canceled—so he had a motive to murder Strickland. But who had a motive to murder Mort? The only question I don't have is whether or not both men were murder victims. That seems pretty clear to me, even if it doesn't to Harris and the police."

Meg ran her hands through her short dark hair. "Andy says the preliminary autopsy report shows Mort Carmody died of a heart attack. His liver was almost completely cirrhosed. He had spots on his lungs from all that smoking. The guy was already one of the walking dead *before* he sat in the hot sun swilling gin."

"Someone could have put something in the orange juice to kick the heart attack off," Quill insisted.

John leaned back on his stool and folded his arms behind his head. "They should have run all kinds of tests for poisons, Quill. But they'll stop, now that Harris has closed the case. So it's possible that a heretofore-undetected poison did just that. But is it probable? Why would someone want to murder Carmody?"

"I did get a chance to talk to the hacker who's going

to investigate all the guys," Meg said. "I pulled him aside for a few seconds. He should have some good information on all of them as early as tomorrow morning."

"What kinda information can a dishwasher get from a computer?" Doreen demanded.

"Bruce isn't just a dishwasher," Meg said. "He's majoring in computer science at Columbia. He said he could get into the California Department of Motor Vehicles, check on the drivers' licenses, and get their Social Security numbers. Once he has those—" She waved her hands in the air. "All kinds of information comes flying out of the Internet. Bank accounts, criminal histories, divorces and remarriages, births—you name it."

Doreen scowled horribly. "It ain't right."

"It's the twenty-first century," Meg said. "We've all got to get used to it."

"It shouldn't be all that easy, Meg," John said. "Most of those accounts have some pretty heavy-duty defenses."

"Bruce," Meg said with satisfaction, "is majoring in cryptography."

"You said he was in computers," Doreen said. "Not funeral homes."

"Cryptography is code-breaking," Quill added.

"He'll get us a lot of good stuff. I'm positive."

"This is great, guys. We should get organized, here," Quill said. "Now. I've made sort of a preliminary list of items to investigate."

"I'm organized," Meg interrupted cheerfully. "Adela Henry called and ordered a brunch for the second session of the screenwriting seminar tomorrow and that's at the top of my list. Bjarne can't handle a brunch for thirty all by himself."

Quill opened her mouth to remind Meg that two days earlier, Bjarne seemed to be able to cope with the brunch with no problem at all. She glanced at her sister. Meg sat in the rocking chair by the kitchen fireplace. Her thumbs drummed restlessly on her knees. She always made a few sartorial concessions when riding the train to New York; when she came home, she invariably shed whatever she'd been wearing in favor of comfort clothes. But the red bandana she had tied around her neck this morning before she left was still there, and she hadn't changed her khaki trousers for shorts, even though the temperature was still in the eighties.

Quill took a thoughtful bite of carrot cake, and promptly spit it out. "Baking soda! Meg, who made the carrot—"

Doreen drove her elbow into Quill's ribs.

"Ow!"

Doreen glared at her and mouthed, "Hush up!"

Quill was so startled she swallowed the remainder of the carrot cake. It was awful. Whoever made it had substituted baking soda for baking powder.

Oblivious, Meg started to rock back and forth. "Now, John, you were going to check into Strickland's background, and Bland's as well. Did you have any luck?"

John nodded. "It's pretty interesting."

"Did of any this get served to the guests?" Quill mouthed to Doreen.

"Huh?"

Quill lowered her voice to a whisper. "I said did the carrot cake get served to—"

"Heck, no. You think I'm crazy?"

"What *are* you two whispering about?" Meg brought the rocking chair forward with a crash and leaped to her feet. "You know what? I'm hot. I'm going to get out of these clothes. I don't know why I didn't change before. Don't plan a thing until I get back!"

Quill watched her sister bounce through the swinging doors to the dining room. She waited until she was certain that Meg was out of earshot. She looked at John in dismay. "All right. What's going on?"

"Cold feet." Doreen folded her arms and sniffed. "Same thing happened to me with my third. A week before the wedding I took every gol-darned thing in the house and scrubbed it within an inch of its life."

"That doesn't sound so awful," Quill said doubtfully. "It sounds as if you wanted to have things nice for your . . . your *third,* Doreen?"

"Pretty near destroyed my whole collection of Lawrence Welk."

"You scrubbed your CDs?"

"Records," she corrected. "Like I said, cold feet."

Quill got up. "It's serious if it's affecting her cooking. Maybe I should go talk to her. You know, Andy thought something might be wrong. Oh. Maybe we should take a look at those news articles you brought from Syracuse, John. We could easily overlook a blackmail opportunity."

"It'll keep."

Quill went through the empty dining room, then up the stairs to Meg's rooms.

Meg hadn't really moved back in after they'd sold the Palate back to Marge; most of her off time had been spent in Andy's cottage near the clinic. Quill tapped at the door and opened it.

Of all the things she didn't want in her rooms, Meg had said when they'd first bought the Inn, a kitchen was at the top of the list. She had a small refrigerator, a one-burner stove, and an eighteen-inch sink tucked in the corner of the living area. The rest of the large room—which overlooked the Falls—was lined with bookcases filled with cookbooks, filing cabinets of recipes, and posters of famous restaurants. A large worktable with a computer occupied the middle of the room; a long davenport was shoved against one long end, set to face the view.

Meg's bedroom door was half-open. Meg herself was nowhere in sight.

"Meg?"

No answer.

"Meggie?"

Meg rose from her prone position on the davenport and peered over the back at Quill.

"Hey," Quill said.

"Hey yourself."

"Can I make you some coffee?"

"You make awful coffee."

"This is true. Can I offer sisterly comfort?"

Meg crossed her eyes, stuck out her tongue, and fell backward. Quill walked around to the front of the couch, swept the copies of *Gourmet* and *L'Aperitif* off the coffee table, and sat on it. Meg stared up at the ceiling.

"Doreen says you have cold feet about the wedding."

Meg sighed.

"She says the exact same thing happened to her with her third."

"Her third?"

"Yep."

"Stoke is her fourth husband, right?"

"Right."

"I wonder what happened to all the others?"

"I've never asked her." Quill thought a minute. "I'd like to know. Why don't you ask her?"

"Because I'm fond of the teeth I've got."

"She wouldn't hit you with a broom."

"She's hit me with a broom before."

"She's hit each of us with a broom before. I think you're in an exempt stage, though. You're a bride. Or about to be."

Meg didn't answer.

"I can't tell you to get married or not get married, Meg, because I have a stake in the outcome. But I can *listen* fairly objectively. I think."

"I love Andrew."

"He's a lovable guy."

"Why *do* people get married, Quill? The first time around I was in love, I was young, and we wanted children. Then, when Simon was killed, all that went up in flames." Her voice quavered a little. "Literally. You pulled me out of that horrible abyss I fell into after Simon's death, by dragging me here. We took all our savings and decided we were going to make it. And we did. Or sort of. I mean, we haven't had to declare bankruptcy or anything. Not yet, anyhow," she added with what Quill felt was a callous disregard for her feelings. She was, after all the finance person. Sort of.

"And you received the four-star rating from *L'Aperitif.*" She leaned over and punched Meg lightly in the arm. "And?"

"And I like it. I like getting up in the morning and going down to the kitchen I designed and bossing all the Finnish sous-chefs around and making great, fantastic, terrific, wonderful food. I like going out to my garden and picking herbs to use at lunch. I love the sound of the Falls, and the way snow looks in the early morning at Christmastime."

"What about the bright lights and the big city?" Quill said, surprised. "I thought you loved being on Lally Preston's TV show, and taking over the kitchen at La Strazza from Anatole Spineless—"

"Supinsky."

"Whatever. Anyhow . . ."

Meg sat up and drummed her heels on the plank flooring. "I hate New York! I hate the air! I hate the crowds! I hate the weaselly little backstabbing pastry chef at La Strazza who'd as soon put baking soda into the baking powder as look at you!"

"About the baking-soda thing, Meg . . ."

"Every kitchen in New York has *cockroaches!*" Meg yelled. "Because cockroaches outlast human beings and you can't get *rid of them*! You just coexist! With cockroaches!" She flopped back on the couch, scowling like a gargoyle. "Andy loves New York, and the career opportunity at Columbia is fabulous. Fabulous. There is no way he can do the kind of research here in Hemlock Falls that he can do there, Quill. And I can get all the publicity and attention my career needs right here in Hemlock Falls. In a setting Anatole would kill for."

"Well . . ." Quill said doubtfully.

"Oh, yes he would!" Meg's face was pink. She gave the floor a final thump and demanded, "Do you know what I found at La Strazza this afternoon?"

"Cockroaches?"

"A letter and a résumé from Anatole Supinksy. Addressed to you! He wants my job here, the little Hungarian rat!"

"I thought he was in Budapest."

"He got off the plane before it took off," Meg said briefly. "What am I going to do, Quill? Andy's so excited about this move. He keeps finding wonderful apartments, and I keep finding cockroaches."

"Yikes," Quill said. "Well, would Andy live here and commute home on weekends?"

"If I asked him to, sure. But I don't think I can. You know what the research life is like, Quill. He has to be there, on call, all the time. It'd drive him nuts, traveling back and forth."

"At least you want to get married," Quill said wryly.

"Of course I want to get married. Don't you want to get married?"

"No," Quill said frankly. "I don't."

Meg ignored this. "I've tried to get excited about New York, Quill, but I can't. I just can't. And when I got to La Strazza today and found that letter . . . aaaghh! It hit me. It hit me! I'm planning to walk into the hell of the La Strazza kitchen while Anatole is *stealing my job here!*"

Quill grabbed her ankle. "Stop *thumping,* Meg." She held on to Meg's shoe while she thought. "There must be a solution."

"You're grinning."

"I am?" Quill said, surprised. "I'm happy you don't want to leave."

"Then you can let go of my shoe."

Quill let go. "You have to talk with Andy about this."

"I can't. He'll go noble on me and give up the Columbia clinic. He can't give up the Columbia clinic. I just have to move to New York and lump it."

"We'll think of something," Quill said. "I promise you we'll think of something."

"Like what? I've thought and thought and I can't think of a thing except that one of us has to commute. And it's too hard on Andy. I can take it. I don't have to be on call. I'm not the one who'll be getting phone calls at three in the morning about dying little kids. The only work-related calls I'd get at three in the morning are because the snails are crawling all over the Sub-Zero because someone didn't screw the lid to the jar on tight."

"I did, too, screw the lid on," Quill said crossly. "That happened *years* ago, Meg, and you're never going to forget it, are you?"

Meg lay back on the couch and folded her hands on her stomach. "Probably not," she agreed comfortably. "Go away. I have to think some more."

Quill went into the kitchen in a much better frame of mind, to find Doreen gone, Max asleep on his back by the fireplace, and John paging through a thick file folder. He looked up and smiled. "She's okay."

"You can tell just from looking at me? Yes, she's okay. A little frazzled, but not depressed. She doesn't want to move to New York."

"Will Andy commute?"

"She says she won't ask him to. She'll work it out, John. I'm just glad that . . ." She blinked back tears.

"You really thought she was going to march off into the sunset without a word? You know your sister better than that."

"I should have, I suppose." She settled into the rocking chair, absurdly happy. "So, what news on the Rialto?"

"Would you like the long version or the short?"

"Maybe just the relevant parts?"

Max groaned and twitched in his sleep. Suddenly he woke, craned his neck over his withers and scrambled to his feet. He stood at attention, floppy ears pricked forward. Then he threw his head back and howled. The back of Quill's neck prickled with fear. "What's wrong, boy? That's a stupid question, isn't it? Be quiet, Max."

John stared up at the ceiling. "What room is Ed Schwartz staying in?"

Quill stood frozen. "Two-ten," she whispered. "Two-ten. Right over our heads."

CHAPTER 13

"Nothing!" Quill said with relief. "What the heck is the matter with you, Max?" She'd used the skeleton key to open the door. The room was empty. John looked in the closet and in the small bath. Max circled the floor, sniffing eagerly. She'd always liked the colors in two-ten; the bedspread and the drapes were a tea-stained chintz patterned with soft pink hydrangea. Ed's suitcase was open and the clothes carelessly stuffed into it. A pile of manuscripts was stacked carelessly on the small Louis XIV–style desk. Max howled, and dashed out the door.

John raced after him; Quill hobbled along behind. There were fire escapes at either end of the long hall. Max dashed toward the one at the south end. He sat in front of the fire door and howled dismally.

"It's a woodchuck," Quill said, her heart pounding.

"Or a raccoon. One climbed the stairs last year, remember?"

John pushed at the bar. "There's something behind it. Stay here, Quill, I'll go outside and come up."

"It's not Ed," Quill said to Max as she waited. The dog sniffed eagerly at the door, then began to bark. "It isn't Ed."

It was Ed.

Andy closed the door to the hospital room carefully behind him. "Massive whack to the head. Subdural hematoma to those of you not familiar with medical terminology."

Quill stood close to John. Both of them were leaning against the clinic walls. Quill was too tired to move. Benny Gilpin chewed his lips nervously. Meg stared at Andy, then asked, "Did he say who hit him?"

"He's in a coma. It's a grade three. If I'm any judge of such things, he'll probably come out of it tomorrow. We're monitoring the hemorrhage with CAT scans. I don't think we'll have to open his skull to relieve the pressure. If we do, I'll need to notify next of kin."

"He's got a son and daughter in Tacoma," Benny said. He picked restlessly at a scab on his forearm. "I can track the boy down, probably. His name's Ronald, I think. Where is that jerk Harris?"

"He's been notified," Andy said. "If you'll excuse me, I'm going down to the lab. His blood samples should be ready to read. Coming with me, Meg?"

She shook her head. "I'll stay here, Andy."

"And I'm staying with you guys," Benny said. He looked desperately at John. "Mind if I bunk in with

you tonight, Raintree? That Harris ought to offer pro-
tection, but those clowns don't seem to know their ass
from a hole in the ground. I mean, people are dying
here!"

"Little nervous?" John asked.

"Who the hell wouldn't be!" Benny exploded.

"It should be all over tomorrow." John folded his
arms, his face expressionless.

"What d'ya mean?"

"If Ed regains consciousness, he'll be able to iden-
tify who hit him. And all this will be over."

"It could be over sooner if you told us why Mort
was going to blackmail Neil Strickland."

"I don't know!" Benny's eyes welled with tears.
"Whatever was going on, I wasn't in on it. Ed wanted
to cut me in, and I said no way, pally. I've kept my
nose clean for too many years to get screwed up now."

Quill was getting tired of the language, and even
more tired of Benny himself. "I don't believe you,"
she said coolly. "I don't think any of us believe you."

"Why won't you believe me?"

Despite herself, Quill felt a pang of sympathy. The
guy was terrified, there was no faking that. But was he
terrified because he was innocent, and threatened with
harm over something he knew nothing about? "*Ten
Little Indians,*" she said.

"Ten little what?!"

"It's that Agatha Christie story," Meg said. "*And
Then There Were None*. You're the last one left. If you
didn't kill Strickland and Carmody, who did? Not Ed
Schwartz, unless he laid his own skull open."

"There's that bastard Bland," Benny said. His eyes

darted from one to the other. "He's the focal point of all this."

"Small problem with that, bozo," Meg said. "He was in Los Angeles when Neil Strickland was killed, remember? And he flew out to Chicago from Ithaca late this afternoon."

"Maybe he didn't make the plane!"

"Twice?" John asked dryly.

"Okay. Fine. You three want to suspect me, you go right ahead. All I have to say is this: I'm not staying at your goddamn Murder Inn another night!"

"Murder Inn," Quill said ruefully an hour later. She, Meg, and John sat on her balcony. Meg was drinking a glass of wine. Quill sipped at a glass of sun tea. The sunset had been dark; thunderheads gathered to the east. An occasional strike of lightning lit the sky. "We don't seem to be able to keep the guests healthy, that's for sure."

"I just hope Horvath doesn't back out." Meg swirled the Cabernet in her glass, then swallowed appreciatively. "You couldn't blame him. Up till now, he's had a pretty good impression of America."

"You didn't see the cartoon show Benny wrote. Well, Benny, Ed, and Mort, I suppose."

"It didn't seem to bother him too much," Meg said.

"You're kidding, right? He may have been on his company manners in front of all those other would-be screenwriters, but he certainly was upset when he showed it to me! Why do you think I was drinking vodka with him?"

Meg shrugged. "I don't know. Good guest relations? Anyway, he didn't see it at the workshop for the first time, Quill. Dina, Doreen, and I showed it to him."

"You showed it to him? When?" John asked.

"Friday, I think it was. Dina was all upset about it, and she didn't want him to be embarrassed if someone asked him about it, so we took him into your office and used that VCR. He thought it was funny." She shook her head. "Finns. I'll never understand their sense of humor."

"This absolutely doesn't compute." Quill reached down and scratched futilely at her cast. Even with the new-style bandages, it itched like a giant mosquito bite. "He said he was blindsided when the guys showed the cartoon at the workshop. He wanted me to throw them out!"

"And you didn't," Meg said. She swigged her wine. "Just think, if you'd thrown Ed out, the poor guy's head would have been bashed in at the Holiday Inn."

Quill took the glass from Meg's hand and set it on the small cocktail table. "Enough. You ought to go to bed."

Meg yawned hugely. "You're right. I'm off. This is me, getting up."

"You're not driving over to Andy's, are you?"

"Would I be swilling this indifferent cab if I were? Not. He's on third shift at the clinic, so he's sleeping there tonight. And I? I'm for me own little bed." She dropped a light kiss on John's head, then gave Quill a hug. "I'll see you all in the morning."

"Take an aspirin before you go to sleep!" Quill called after her. She waited until her front door slammed. Her eyes met John's. "Horvath?" she said, disbelieving. "Horvath is behind the murders?"

"It seems unlikely," John admitted. "What possible motive could he have?"

"I don't know. But you know what they say."

"What who says?"

Quill waved her hand vaguely in the air. "Policemen. Half the time motive isn't a factor in finding and convicting a criminal. Means and opportunity are more relevant."

"We're a bit stuck as far as the means, Quill. From the look of it, poor Schwartz was hit by a sledgehammer. But he'll be able to tell us more when he comes to."

"I hope Harris follows up on that guard he promised for the hospital room."

"If he doesn't—and it's unlikely that Harris would do anything to jeopardize his upward career path at this stage—I guess that Andy will keep an eye out."

"He's an awfully good person, John."

"Is Meg backing out?"

"No." Quill tried to bring her knees up to her chest, but the cast wouldn't fit on the chair edge. Besides, it hurt. "But I have a guess about what will happen."

"And?"

"I think she'll put the wedding off. It didn't seem all that well planned anyway," she added plaintively. "Where were they planning to have it? The Tompkins County courthouse? With good old Bernie Bristol presiding?"

"They were planning to have it here, on the terrace. With Dookie officiating."

"She hadn't invited any of her friends. She hadn't even invited me!"

"They wanted an impromptu ceremony. They were going to call their friends a few days before and ask them to drop by. Both of them have been married before."

"Andy has? I didn't know that."

"An early marriage, in med school. He and his wife were both residents when they decided to call it quits." He laughed a little. "Now, where were you?"

"Where? Oh! She'll put it off."

"How will Andy—never mind. You're undoubtedly right, Quill. But it doesn't seem quite fair, does it?"

"Fair to whom? It's marriage that isn't fair, John. Any sort of law that tries to control the relationships between people is screwy." She could feel his eyes on her in the dark. She cleared her throat. "Don't you think so?"

"Maybe," he said.

"You think that's an unsophisticated way to look at it. But let's take all the property-owning issues out of it. What's left?"

She could feel him shrug in the dark. "I suppose it depends on your point of view."

She tugged at her hair. He rose and went to the balcony's edge. The moon sailed high and white in the dark. "I'd better turn in." She could almost feel him smile. "You've started to pull your hair."

She stopped tugging. "What will happen if we"—she hesitated, searching for the right words—"just remain friends?"

"Is that all you want from a man? Friendship? It's

not all I want from a woman. What will happen will happen to both of us. You'll be lonely. You'll find someone to be with. And you'll stop being lonely. So will I."

"Ha," Quill said in a meditative way. She felt vaguely insulted.

"The lovelorn suitor is for Victorian romances, Quill." John's voice was matter-of-fact. "Adult love, good love, is all about exchanges. Communication. Being together every day. It's not about misunderstandings. The magic in love isn't the unspoken or the unknown. It's the dailiness of it." He dropped a kiss on the top of her head, as fraternal as Meg's had been sisterly.

She sat for a long time on the balcony, picking at the knot of this most terrible of questions: whom do I love and why? The moon floated in the sky like a silver buoy. Something rustled in the bushes. She yawned, and went to bed.

She dreamed she was back in the gym, and that the Gravitron landed on her foot and made it hurt like anything.

She woke up and stared at the ceiling, collecting her scattered wits. She wiggled her toes. Her foot felt like a hot balloon spiked with needles. She'd been doing effortless chin-ups in her dream, the Gravitron pulling her lightly up, lightly down, and the Gravitron was somehow mixed up with John, and then the tread slammed upward, just missing her chin, and for some reason this all related to the pain in her broken toes.

She sighed and got out of bed. Max gave a questioning whine and Quill bent and patted him. She straightened up with a groan. Andy had suggested a painkiller, and she'd turned it down. He'd also suggested cold packs to keep the swelling down, and she'd forgotten all about it. But who could have imagined toes would hurt like the very devil? Quill hobbled to the bathroom and snapped on the light. She rummaged through the medicine cabinet. There was all that herbal stuff from Sherri Kerri's gym. Any full-blooded, worth-its-salt herbal fitness program ought to have an herbal remedy for pain; there were the usual muscle aches from exercise, not to mention all those people who fell off treadmills . . .

And the people who got smacked with the Gravitron.
Quill sat down on the bathtub, heart pounding. She ran through a mental list.

1. Neil Strickland was dressed for a workout when he left the Inn at quarter to four.

2. Mort Carmody had followed Neil.

3. Max had followed Mort; Mort's denim shirt was in his jaws on the day of the murder.

4. Mort had died from an unknown agent that had precipitated a heart attack. Sherri had such an agent in her pharmacopoeia. Sherri could have made a good guess about Mort's physical status, too. That gray-faced, blue-lipped look was a notorious indicator of heart trouble.

5. Twenty-four hours after Strickland's death, Mort was in business with Sherri Kerri—

and she'd claimed that she never wanted a partner the first time Quill met her.

6. Mort had been blackmailing Sherri over Neil's death.

7. Sherri was at the Inn when Mort died. She could have slipped the Vita Life into the orange juice.

8. Sherri Kerri was the perp. There was the matter of Sherri's knowledge about the resort. She had known, why else would she make an offer for the Inn? Who'd told her? Mort? Quill decided this didn't matter, and tossed it aside.

"Wow," Quill said to her image in the mirror. "Wow." But why attack Ed? And Benny? Well, no one had attacked Benny. Yet. Was Meg right? Was this truly a murder marinade? Could the attack on Ed—and Benny's fear—be due to something else? Someone else?

Quill thought about Horvath. This deal was important to the Finns, that was clear. And with the resort going up, there was going to be a lot of money floating around Hemlock Falls. With Mort dead, was Horvath taking advantage of the aura of violence and dispatching Finn-insulting scriptwriters for God and country?

Quill swallowed two ibuprofen tablets and hobbled into her living room. She sat down on the couch and switched on the lamp. Max pattered in from the bedroom and went to the front door. He whined and pawed it.

"No, Max."

He barked.

"Stop it, Max!" The knock was faint, so faint that Quill couldn't believe she heard it. "John?" she asked. She went to the door and opened it.

"Hello!" Sherri said cheerfully. "I saw your light. Glad you were up."

Quill didn't really believe you could see madness. You could see the effects of madness—the drugs people took to stave off voices, the emotions stirred by manic surges of energy—but your average, everyday madwoman had a face no different from those of her saner sisters.

And Sherri looked just fine.

Quill backed toward the phone. Tompkins County didn't have 911. But John's extension was just three digits. If she could get to the phone. "It's two o'clock in the morning, Sherri."

"I know it's two o'clock in the morning." She wore a sleeveless T-shirt. Quill could see the muscles under the tanned skin. "Two o'clock in the morning seems to be the only time you aren't surrounded by people. Hello, Max!"

Max wagged his tail. Sherri scratched under his chin. So much for dog love. "You want to watch, Max?"

Quill's skin crawled. She leaned against the wall, and fell into the umbrella stand. Sherri extended her arms and flexed her muscles.

"What's going on here?" Quill said firmly. If she could get to the kitchen, she could get to a knife.

"You-u-u sa-a-a-w meee!" Sherri sang. "Na-a-aughty!"

"Saw you what?" Ed's red ponytail, she thought. The same color as my hair. Sherri was trying to kill me, not Ed.

"Kissing Mr. Bland."

"Mr. Bland? The man you were kissing in the gym was Mr. Bland? I don't care if you want to kiss Mr. Bland," Quill expostulated. "You can kiss lawyers all you want."

The red minivan. Sherri was trying to kill *me*.

"Kissing Daddy."

The room turned icy.

"Everett Bland? Everett Bland's your father?" Quill whispered. Her heart ached with pity.

"Kissing Daddy."

And then she came for her.

CHAPTER 14

"You had to hit Max with an umbrella to make him jump Sherri?" Meg said. "Thank God you *had* an umbrella! More coffee? Don't move! I'll pour it for you."

Quill adjusted her foot so the sun didn't fall directly on the cast. They were sitting on the flagstone terrace. Everyone had fussed over her in an extremely embarrassing way. "If I hadn't hit him with the umbrella, he would have watched Sherri strangle me," Quill rasped. She rubbed her throat.

"Have some more honey lemonade." Meg poured from the pitcher on the table and added ice. She frowned over the mint leaves in the chilled bowl and tossed them aside. "The leaves are wilting. They've been in the sun too long."

"The taste is still okay, though."

"Stop talking, Quill. It makes my eyes water. Andy

says there's damage to your larynx, but it shouldn't be permanent. He hopes."

"What about Sherri? How permanent is her damage?"

"God, Quill. They've got the death penalty in New York now."

"It's Bland they should lock up."

"Stop talking. I'll do the talking. Yes, they should lock Bland up. But they can't. Sherri won't bring charges."

Quill gurgled.

"Bland denies everything." Meg held her hand up. "I know. I know. Sherri kept trying to explain to Myles why she had to kill you. So we all know what you saw. God, Quillie." Meg's face was pale. She put her hands over her eyes for a moment. "She is crazy, you know. It must have driven her clean out of her mind. She says it started when she was eight. Sorry, kiddo. I shouldn't have told you."

They sat for a moment in the sunshine.

"The saddest thing is, Strickland's death was an accident. He came for the free workout, and wouldn't listen to her about how to use the Gravitron. So it smacked him in the chin and killed him. Mort walked in just in time to see it happen. Sherri was petrified that she'd lose her gym if someone died there, so Mort helped her dispose of the body in the gorge, and they both decided to pin it on Max."

Max, stretched out in the cool of the flagstone, thumped his tail at the sound of his name.

"You were right about how she killed Mort. *If* she killed Mort. There's no way to prove it, and the tests are all coming back negative for all the stuff that was in the herbal supplement. There aren't any murders at all, Quill. Just improper body disposal and an assault on Ed Schwartz."

"But she'll be tried, won't she?"

"Don't talk! Yes. But Howie said this morning that if he were handling the defense, he'd plead diminished responsibility."

Quill waved at the men staking out land on the other side of the Gorge. She could just make out the glint of Simon's gold beard.

"Oh, yeah. You were right about that, too. The mega-resort. Bland told his daughter about it, of course, and she set her gym business up here because there's going to be a boom. JoyMax is the principal investor, and the only people with more money than they have are those Silicon Valley guys. The resort is going to be huge, Quill. They're talking about a sort of Disney World north. I thought Doreen was just being silly, but she was right. There's going to be a ton of money coming into Hemlock Falls. Maybe two tons."

Quill smiled and nodded a question at her.

"Andy and me? Well, there's this huge clinic going in, of course. A place as large as this one is going to need a lot of services. So Andy is going into partnership at the clinic with the new guys, and he's going to do research at Cornell. So he'll commute, for only twenty minutes!"

Quill tapped her ice cubes.

"Right. It's very cool. Let's see, what else? Oh. Benny Gilpin beat feet out of town and never came back. Who knows what happened to him? For that matter, who cares? Mort was blackmailing someone all right, but it was Sherri, not Neil Strickland."

Quill made the sort of noises one makes in a dentist's chair during root-canal work.

"Myles came back right away, as soon as he heard you were hurt. You might not remember, but he visited you in the hospital yesterday. Andy had you pretty drugged up." She tugged on her lower lip. "John spent the night outside your hospital room in a chair. And Doreen went and put potpourri in your room so it will smell great all day."

Quill nodded and drank some lemonade. Meg had used honey instead of sugar. She wished she had some mint. It tasted better when it wasn't totally perfect.

Meg was so upset by the marinade of events in her life that August that she substituted baking soda for baking powder in her recipe for carrot cake. She borrowed the recipe from Josephine DiChario, who was totally bummed out at the mistake.

JOSEPHINE'S BAKING POWDER
CARROT CAKE

2 cups flour
1 1/2 cups sugar
2 teaspoons baking powder
2 teaspoons cinnamon
1 cup canola oil
4 large eggs
2 cups shredded carrots
1 eight-ounce can drained, crushed pineapple
1 cup of chopped pecans
1 cup flaked fresh coconut
1 cup plump raisins

Mix flour, sugar, baking powder, cinnamon together.
Make a well in the center and put oil and eggs in
well. Beat until completely blended. Add remaining
ingredients and bake at 350 degrees in two floured
cake pans for 35 to 40 minutes.

Frosting: 1 eight-ounce package of cream cheese, 4
tablespoons unsalted butter, 1 ½ teaspoons of freshly
grated orange peel, and 3 cups of confectioners
sugar.

Visit Claudia Bishop's Web site address at
www.mysteryhouse.com

EARLENE FOWLER

introduces Benni Harper, curator of San Celina's folk
art museum and amateur sleuth

❑ **FOOL'S PUZZLE**   **0-425-14545-X/$6.50**

Ex-cowgirl Benni Harper moved to San Celina, California, to
begin a new career as curator of the town's folk art museum. But
when one of the museum's first quilt exhibit artists is found dead,
Benni must piece together a pattern of family secrets and small-
town lies to catch the killer.

❑ **IRISH CHAIN**   **0-425-15137-9/$6.50**

When Brady O'Hara and his former girlfriend are murdered at the
San Celina Senior Citizen's Prom, Benni believes it's more than
mere jealousy—and she risks everything to unveil the conspiracy
O'Hara had been hiding for fifty years.

❑ **KANSAS TROUBLES**   **0-425-15696-6/$6.50**

After their wedding, Benni and Gabe visit his hometown near
Wichita. There Benni meets Tyler Brown: aspiring country singer,
gifted quilter, and former Amish wife. But when Tyler is murdered
and the case comes between Gabe and her, Benni learns that her
marriage is much like the Kansas weather: bound to be stormy.

❑ **GOOSE IN THE POND**   **0-425-16239-7/$6.50**
❑ **DOVE IN THE WINDOW**   **0-425-16894-8/$6.50**